CW00657119

No Small Stir

By

Phil Hadley

© Phil Hadley 2017

All rights reserved. No part of this publication may be reproduced or transmitted in any form or by any means, electronic or mechanical, including photocopy, recording, or any information storage and retrieval system without the prior written permission of the copyright holder.

Phil Hadley hereby asserts and gives notice of his right under s.77 of the Copyright, Designs & Patents Act 1988 to be identified as the author of this work.

ISBN 978 1 9998463 0 5

Printed on recycled paper

Printed by
R Booth Ltd, Penryn, Cornwall.

Dedicated

to my awesome son

&

in memory of a loving sister

Ruth Hadley

1956-2017

Missionary to Angola 1982-2017

ACKNOWLEDGEMENTS

Thanks to my late parents for enthusing me with a love of history, to my History teacher for taking seriously my passion for tales of the Second World War, and to those family and friends who have encouraged this journey into print over a number of years.

Thank you to Harvey Graver for his amazing artwork for the cover and for Anne & Maria Squires for the design.
Do visit their studio, tea-room & guest house in Veryan.

With deep gratitude to the generation that served in the Second World War for the freedom we enjoy today and especially those that made the ultimate sacrifice defeating the evils of extremism.
"At the going down of the sun and in the morning
we will remember them."
Laurence Binyon "For The Fallen", The Times, September 1914

"If the present tries to sit in judgement of the past,

it will lose the future.

Criticism is easy; achievement is difficult."

Sir Winston Churchill 1874-1965

PROLOGUE

The first streaks of sunlight danced on the ripples of the rising tide. They gave a sparkling effect that made the surface of the water appear silver. The gently rising currents lapped the rocks that formed the shoreline of the creek. An old oak, its lower boughs arched just above the water, stood on the edge of the crag. The banks of the whole creek were wooded creating a scene of tranquillity, of serenity, of silence. Nothing stirred, just the gentle lap, lap, lap of the water as the tide began once more to cover the mud that had this airing twice a day.

Perhaps it was the song of the skylark as it hovered high above the water, perhaps it was a shaft of sunlight as it penetrated through the leaves of the overhanging limb, perhaps it was the movement of the dinghy as the water began to lift it off the bottom, he wasn't sure, but something caused Johann to open his eyes. He gently rubbed them trying to take in his surroundings. Trees, sky, water. For a moment he was back on the lake in the Harz Mountains as a boy. He had spent many a holiday with his grandparents, fishing, climbing trees, hiking. His grandfather had worked in the Grube Samson installing a power station, fallen in love with the area and bought a little woodsman's cottage on the shores of the Oderteich. Johann loved the summers he had spent exploring the lake, the woods, the old mine workings down the valley. He frowned as he struggled to comprehend how he had been transported back to his childhood idyll.

Johann sat up with a jolt. He gasped. This wasn't Lower Saxony, and as he surveyed the scene before him in the dinghy it certainly wasn't any childhood paradise. Hans lay motionless sprawled over the front of the dinghy. An arm dangled down into the water. His clothes were still sodden from his time in the water. Johann reached for a wrist. He was looking for a pulse but the hand felt cold and clammy as he held it and pushed the cuff back. It was all coming back to him now. They were rowing, rowing frantically to avoid the ship that was looming out of the darkness. As it towered above them, Hans had looked up, but had lost his balance and fallen into the water. There was no pulse. His lips looked an odd shade of purple. He was dead. Johann let go of his wrist and the arm flopped lifelessly to the floor of the dinghy. Hans must have been in the water for an hour before they managed to locate him.

He was face down, and Johann remembered the struggle to haul his sodden frame into the dinghy.

He turned to look at Siegfried. Daylight meant he saw for the first time just what had happened last night. As Hans had fallen into the water, Siegfried had stood up in the dinghy and with his bare hands had tried to push them away from the vast hulk of the ship that had threatened to swamp them. The vessel wasn't doing many knots but the speed was enough for the contact to jar, for Siegfried to fall banging his head on the hull, and then to land mercifully in the bottom of the dinghy. He had spent the next hour moaning and groaning while Johann tried to quieten him, all the time rowing around looking for Hans. Eventually they had bumped into him floating in the darkness, and hauled him aboard. This had brought more groans from Siegfried. Johann remembered rowing for all he was worth trying to get up the estuary into the narrower part of the river where there would be some cover where they could assess the situation in the light of day. He didn't remember rowing into the creek, but exhaustion must have overtaken him, and tide and current combined to deposit them on their present resting place.

Siegfried had received a nasty blow to the head. There was a dent in part of his skull and his hair was matted with blood. Johann reached out and touched Siegfried on the arm. There was a sudden intake of breath, but he didn't open his eyes.

"At least he's still alive," thought Johann. "But for how long? He needs a doctor and a hospital and sooner rather than later." Johann knelt over him and looked for any other injuries. He couldn't see any, but then the one he could see was bad enough.

"I'll have to go for help," he thought. "There must be a cottage or a house somewhere." Then another scene flashed into his mind. He was in an office at 76 Tirpitzufer, Berlin. It was the Headquarters of the Abwehr. It was the Colonel's office. The Colonel was in charge of Abwehr II – the department responsible for sending agents into enemy territory to commit acts of sabotage and collect intelligence. Even now he could hear the Colonel's words:

"The mission… the mission is all important. Should one of you be killed, the rest carry on. Completion of the mission is vital. The success of our plans to invade

England is riding on your shoulders. Cornwall is of strategic importance if we are to stop the English calling on their Empire for reinforcements. That is why you have been handpicked for the task. Remember, the mission is all important."

Johann ran his hand back through his blonde hair. He always did this when he was thinking, when he had to weigh up a situation and decide what to do. "If I leave Siegfried here he will die. If I go for help, we will be captured and the mission will fail." He sighed deeply. Every ounce of his humanity was crying out for him to do the best for Siegfried. Every ounce of his training and his devotion to his country was crying out for him to rise to his duty.

Hans was beyond helping. "But I can give Siegfried a chance," he thought as he reached into his coat and fumbled for the small first aid kit they had been issued with. He took out a wound dressing, gently placed it over the concave hollow on the temple of the motionless Siegfried. He wound the bandage round as best he could to keep it in place, tying it off neatly. "Grandmother will be pleased with that one," he said to himself. He was grateful for the evenings by the fire in the cottage by the lake where she had made him practice. He thought back to the time he had fallen and cut himself and had limped back. She had told him "If you are out exploring by yourself, you need to know how to look after yourself." She had been a nurse in the Great War and so over a series of summers had passed on some of her skills to her adventurous grandson. "You never know when you might need to do this," he heard her telling him. He was grateful he had listened.

"That should give Siegfried an extra hour or two," Johann reasoned with himself. "Hopefully he will be found soon. A forester, or even a poacher. Anybody who can get help."

The dinghy was now afloat once more as the tide continued to fill the creek. Johann picked up an oar and began to paddle. He was looking for somewhere where he could get out and leave his companions to their fate. "If Siegfried is going to be found, I need to be as far away from here as possible. The mission… the mission is all important." He thought back to the daring of the U-boat captain who had seized the opportunity to shadow a minesweeper as she came into Falmouth. They couldn't believe their luck as the harbour boom was opened and they were able to get right inside. The pluck of the wily submariner had overcome one of the more hazardous parts of their getting ashore. Then under the cover of darkness in what was marked on the charts as St Just Pool they had just poked the hatch above the surface while the three of them slipped out and into the dinghy, had waved a final thank you to the U-boat and rowed up the River Fal. The U-boat was hoping another vessel would leave harbour that night and they could slip through the boom undetected. It would be long gone by now. No hope of calling it back. No hope of rescue.

Johann rowed on past a tree that looked like it was dipping its leathery fingers into the creek. As the shoreline curved round there were two granite gateposts standing as if on sentry duty. As the dinghy came closer Johann soon decided this was an ideal place for the parting of the ways. In times past this was obviously some kind of access down to the water's edge. Now he could step out of the dinghy with no fear of leaving footprints in the mud. Although the tide was still rising he didn't know how far it would come before it turned and he couldn't risk having his escape exposed for Siegfried's rescuers to discover.

Johann stepped ashore. He gave the dinghy a gentle push and said a silent farewell to its occupants. He turned and walked up the slope. Just a few yards brought him to a trackway that ran under the trees. "Right or left," he pondered. "Left will take me back along the river. I want to get inland, so it must be right."

He walked at a brisk pace. He wanted to run but he thought that would be more suspicious if he was spotted. He kept going. He didn't know it but those that lived in these parts called it 'The Wrinkling Lane'. Soon he was at the top of the creek. He looked back. Silence. Save for the tapping of a woodpecker, and the scurrying of a squirrel. He turned and continued on his way.

Chapter 1

A solitary truck made its way slowly over the long stone bridge. Perhaps it was just the laziness of the late summer afternoon, maybe the driver was taking in the view of the river as it meandered down to the bridge and then broadened as it wended its way northwards to the Atlantic, or perchance he had heard the legend that when first constructed in 1468 by a local reverend it was founded on sacks of wool, and he was a-feared of the state of its foundation with the passage of time. Whichever it may be, the waters swirled under the stone arches as the incoming tide met the waters which had journeyed from the heights of the Cornish moors.

Downstream a small coastal steamer, the Florence of Liverpool, had made its way up from Padstow on the rising tide and was now inching its way into the wharf on the west bank of the river where a couple of Cornwall Farmer's workmen stood watching next to a small line of railway wagons which awaited the ship's cargo.

Upstream the sound of hammers on metal emanated from the engine shed at the railway station as Engine 0298 was in the depot for repair. The lorry disappeared off the bridge and made its way through the short avenue of shops and businesses to the level crossing. The gates were open allowing it to cross freely. The main road through Fore Street stretched up the hill in front of the driver but he turned left onto the Platt. Here on the corner stood a public house which had taken its name from the legend of the bridge. A little further on the right stood the town council offices, sandbagged against blast. An officious looking gentleman emerged from the L shaped barricade in front of the door, placed his bowler hat carefully on his head and strode purposefully across the road. Next door to the town hall the windows of the Co-Op were boarded up. The lorry passed between the Regal cinema and the garage on the opposite side of the road and then halted to allow the doctor in his black car to turn right. The town's physician was returning from a house call on an outlying farm.

The lorry passed some Victorian villas before the hedges closed in and the lane began to rise leaving the town of Wadebridge nestled in the valley behind. The driver turned the bend at Trevanion and had to brake sharply to avoid hitting a young couple walking hand in hand in the middle of the lane. The lorry stopped with about three feet to spare. The startled couple stood aside pressing themselves into the hedge to give the truck room to pass. The driver grated the gears as he struggled to select first to pull away up the slope. With a flourish he acknowledged the couple with a dismissive wave and pulled away. The young man was tall, athletically built with blonde hair. He had what looked like a kit bag over his shoulder with the handle of a small shovel protruding from the drawn strings at the top of the bag. The young woman was considerably shorter with a head of wavy black hair. She looked a year or two younger than her companion and in her cotton summer dress and heeled shoes did not look attired for a countryside ramble.

'Another young lass being taken up lover's lane,' the driver thought to himself as he changed gear and the young couple disappeared from view in his mirror.

'What are the youth of the nation coming to?' he mused to himself. 'Not like my day,' he reminisced of the time when he and his fair maiden had had his Bessy's older sister as a chaperone everywhere they'd gone. 'You could count the kisses I had on one hand before I walked her up the aisle!' and as he pictured each of those romantic occasions the lorry was soon out on the Downs and heading for its destination.

———————

Hester rattled the coal as he shovelled it on the fire. He was not in a good mood. He had exchanged harsh words with his wife before leaving for this all-night shift. He hadn't asked to do it, but Bob the usual fireman had gone sick, and as an ex-soldier he was the fireman at the shed considered most suitable for the duty on the military train. Not that Hester's good lady had understood, especially as he had to leave before the meal she was cooking was ready. But now he was regretting the stern rebuke he gave as he was putting on his boots in the hallway and was taking out his frustration on the shovel in his hand. The armoured train had only arrived at Wadebridge ten days before along with a train crew from the Royal Engineers and a team of gunners from the Tanks Corps. Now Hester was firing up the locomotive ready for a night patrolling on the line between Padstow and Bodmin. The driver was down by the track talking to the shunter about the order of trucks for the train. There would be an armoured truck with a small gun turret in front, followed by a second wagon carrying ammunition. The locomotive would sit in the middle of the train pulling another ammo wagon and armoured truck with gun to the rear. All had been recently painted in a green and brown camouflage pattern. After another shovelful, Hester shut the firebox door, wiped his brow on his sleeve, glanced at the steam pressure gauge, was pleased with the progress shown and so took a breather leaning out the cab to survey the scene in the yard.

It was an hour later when the Holden designed F4 engine began to edge out of Wadebridge on the first run of the evening up to Bodmin General. They would get in a couple of runs along their route before a short pause while the last passenger trains of the day traversed the line. By the time darkness fell at about ten o'clock on this beautiful summer's evening they would have the line to themselves able to support those defending this part of Cornwall against the invasion most expected any day now. If needs be they could switch to the south coast via Bodmin Road and Lostwithiel and take the branch line to Fowey. It would be gone seven o'clock next morning before Hester would walk the short distance up from the station to his small terraced house to face the music. But he put all thought of that out of his mind as he had a job to do. It was up hill all the way to Bodmin and he'd need to keep the firebox well stoked especially as the steepest climb came towards the end of the journey.

The soldiers at either end of the train had tested their modified Hotchkiss turrets. Behind the turret there was an armoured plated wall complete with fire-step and at the top a small embrasure to the front where one of the soldiers acted as look-out peering over the turret. The rest of the men were stood in place behind the armoured plating that gave this train an ungainly appearance.

The driver took the looped token as they passed the Wadebridge East signal box and then crossed onto what appeared to be the down the line. Actually it was a single line up the Camel valley. The 'up' line was in fact the North Cornwall line that ran up the Allen Valley and skirted across the north of the moors to Launceston. The two ran together past Guineaport and the meanderings of the river before separating just before the bridges at Pendavey fooling many a schoolboy or novice train spotter into thinking this was a double line.

Hester shovelled several more loads of coal into the firebox as the driver opened up the engine on what was the straightest section of the line before the valley sides closed in and the line twisted and turned almost as much as the river.

"Nice night for it," said the driver. He was from the Royal Engineers and had been cautious at the prospect of having a civilian fireman on his train. He had become friendlier when he'd learned Hester had served his country in the Great War, and Hester perceived his amiable remark as showing they'd get on alright.

"Aye that be," Hester responded in his North Cornish drawl. The driver was taking in the view of the confluence with Pendavey Farm stood on the headland between the two waters.

On Hester's side of the cab the thinly wooded embankment rose steeply for 50 feet limiting the view. Hester glanced forward along the track towards Pendavey Bridge. Just before the river crossing were the concrete dragon's teeth and other obstructions recently placed at the side of the track to allow them to be swiftly moved to block the line and deny its rapid use to the invader. As his eyes fell back along the track towards the train Hester blinked. He couldn't believe what he saw.

"Brakes!" he yelled. The driver responded instinctively.

"Stop!" Hester shouted as he grabbed the edge of the cab opening bracing himself for impact with one hand whilst releasing steam with a swift action with the other. There was a screech of metal on metal as the brakes bit. The soldiers in the armoured trucks were flung from their perches.

Hester had spotted an iron rod jammed in between the sleepers and the displaced ballast where someone had dug a yard or two of ballast away from under the rail. As the front wheels of the train hit the iron rod as they passed over the unsupported rail it would knock them slightly sidewards causing the train to derail. Hester watched as if in slow motion as the front armoured truck slid towards the hole. They would not stop in time. He could see the danger coming ever closer but could do nothing to avert it. He glanced across at the driver. Their eyes met for a brief second, and the driver would later recall that Hester's face showed the terror of the impending doom.

There was a dreadful shuddering and shaking. The armoured truck had hit the iron bar and lurched to the side. Its wheels had come off the rails and were now tearing across the sleepers with ballast flying in every direction. The squeal of the brakes mingled with the thud, thud, thud as the wheels crossed the sleepers and the cries of the soldiers. The ammunition wagon in front of the engine gave a frightening jolt as it too left the rails. Eventually the whole train slid to a halt. Hester instinctively pulled levers and checked dials to make sure the engine would remain safe. A great cloud of steam arose from the engine almost as if it was sighing with relief now that it had stopped.

Hester and the driver climbed down from the cab to survey the damage. The front wheels of the locomotive were inches from the edge of the cavity below the rail which had begun to buckle under the weight of the armoured truck it had struggled to support. Fortunately the two wagons in front of the engine had not overturned. The concrete sleepers recently placed on this line had probably prevented that. They had been intended to support the heavier trains passing over the route should the Royal Albert Bridge at Saltash be unavailable due to enemy action, but they had saved the armoured train from a far worse calamity. Hester breathed deeply. He had wondered about his chances of survival should one of the ammunition trucks be hit, but had not anticipated sabotage on the line being the greatest threat to his life. He offered up a silent prayer.

"I'll go back to the signal and call the box," said the driver. Hester merely nodded. Men were now clambering out of the armoured truck in all directions. The air became blue with their curses as they took in the scene. One soldier was bleeding from a gash on his head. Another held his arm gingerly. A sergeant, quickly regathering his senses, started barking orders for the wounded to be tended and a check to be made on all the personnel on the train. Those at the rear of the train had escaped with bumps and bruises not having derailed.

After a couple of minutes the driver returned to report assistance was on its way. He took Hester's hand and shook it.

"Well spotted," he said. "If it wasn't for you we'd have hit that at a good speed and God only knows what the result would have been then. Goodness knows what that look out was doing. I think we were meant to have a local man on the train tonight. You've probably prevented there being any loss of life."

Hester blushed feeling the driver's words were rather generous and probably the shock of the situation manifesting itself.

"You did well to respond so quickly," replied Hester.

"What do we do now?" asked the sergeant. "The truck's too heavy for my men to lift back onto the rails."

"They'll send out a crane to do that," smiled Hester. "We simply have to wait for them to get organised and get here."

"Thank you sir," said the sergeant who wheeled around on one foot and then barked, "All round defence, except for the two wounded and Atkins who can keep an eye on them by the train." The men scurried off to take defensive positions that would prevent anyone approaching the train, not that there was a soul to be seen, but someone had visited that spot to sabotage the track and the threat of an ambush was now uppermost in the sergeant's mind.

"Cup of tea," said the driver to Hester. "I've got a flask in the cab assuming it's survived the emergency stop."

"Don't mind if I do," said Hester as the two clambered back into the cab to wait.

The Lieutenant-Colonel threw the report onto his desk in disgust. He looked up at the two officers standing nervously before him.

"Incompetents!" he exclaimed. "If it wasn't for that fireman we would have had a disaster on our hands. Why didn't the lookout see it?" One of the officers opened his mouth to answer and then thought better of it and closed it again. There was a short pause as the Colonel stared at the report on his desk.

"Get me some soldiers on that train who can do the job and who would be capable of stopping Jerry should he come," he said rapping his fingers on the desk.

"I have been making some enquiries, sir." The officer paused waiting for permission to continue.

"Go on," said the Colonel.

"There is a Polish unit who seem to have had some experience on armoured trains. It seems the Poles were quite into this kind of thing."

"Get them!" the Colonel thundered. "They can't be any worse than this shower. The sooner they go back to fixing tanks the better." He nodded at the door and the officer took his cue, saluted and scurried out. The Colonel turned to the other young man in front of him.

"Now what did the civilian police have to say from their enquiries so far on this sabotage of the railway line?"

"Not a lot, sir. The spot, although close to Wadebridge, is quite remote and being in the valley is hidden from the farms either side. They are going back to speak to the farm hands this morning to see if any of them saw anything yesterday afternoon. The five-thirty train from Bodmin Southern Railway station arrived at Wadebridge at six with no mishap, so it seems the damage was done between then and just after seven-thirty when the derailment occurred."

"Very well, keep me posted Harris," replied the Colonel picking up another report on his desk as the signal the meeting was over. The officer saluted and then withdrew.

―――――――

It was almost mid-day as Hester opened the garden gate and walked up the short path towards the front door. He wondered what reception he would get, not only having to leave before last night's meal was ready, but now being late home from his shift as well. He'd been told not to say too much about the happenings of yesterday evening. It had been nine this morning before they'd uncoupled the engine from the trucks in front and been allowed to reverse the remains of the train back to the depot. A crane had been brought down the line from the Exeter depot to lift the trucks back onto the rails and a line gang were at the ready to repair the line as soon as it was clear. But now Hester was feeling hungry and tired.

Before Hester got his hand anywhere near the door knob the door was flung open and a blur of flailing arms and apron engulfed him.

"My dear Hester, my hero," his wife exclaimed as she hugged him. She then held him at arm's length and looked him up and down to make sure he was unscathed.

"Just look at the man who saved the train!" She beamed with pride. "Oh I heard all about it from Mrs Harvey who heard it from her neighbour who's got two of those soldiers billeted on her," she gushed answering Hester's unspoken question. "You'd better come in, dear. You look all in. I've got the kettle on and I'll make you a cup of tea."

Hester smiled and meekly followed her indoors. He was sure he would never fathom out his good lady until his dying day. Such was the lot of a loyal husband.

Chapter 2

The sleek black Humber Snipe pulled up a few yards in front of the Dragon's Teeth. With its six-cylinder engine it had merely purred into sight. The freshly made concrete pimples were being arranged across the road in three staggered lines that prevented any vehicle from passing through. The Captain, who was supervising the platoon of troops, looked up and stepped towards the car as the engine was turned off. The driver's door opened and a figure emerged over the running board. The Captain stood to attention and saluted smartly.

"At ease, Captain," said the new arrival, adjusting his cap onto his closely cropped blond hair. He had only spoken three words but instantly they conveyed a sense of authority – he was wearing the crown insignia of a Major in the British Army upon his battle dress. Yet his voice was also mixed with the gentleness of a Cornishman welcoming a stranger across the threshold of his home. The Cornish accent was just there, soft, but traceable, but had been refined by time spent out of the county. The captain, standing a little shorter than the handsome, athletically built frame in front of him, wondered what form of salutation this might be. But then his military discipline kicked in.

"I'll get the men to move the obstructions, sir. I'm sorry if we have impeded your journey," offered the Captain.

"No need, Captain. They are the very things I've come to see."

"Apologies, Major, I was not expecting an inspection today. Headquarters in Bodmin never said anything when I left this morning." The Captain was sounding a little flustered.

He and his men had only been in the county a little over 24 hours. They'd arrived in a fleet of Western National buses. "Better than an army truck," he'd told his men, but it had reminded him of the stories he'd read as a boy of troops being rushed to the front line in France in the Great War in buses and taxis. It didn't bode well, but the army had had to abandon lots of its vehicles on the roads outside Dunkirk. So Western National Omnibuses were called into service to ferry troops preparing the defence of Britain. Still, it was better than marching. When the green boneshakers had finally pulled up to the barracks in Bodmin, the Captain and his men were sent a couple of miles out of town to a tented camp amongst the trees above Lanhydrock House, a large Jacobean mansion that was the home of Viscount Clifden. The camp had been hastily erected to provide shelter for the hordes of the British Expeditionary Force returning bedraggled from France to the Cornish ports of Falmouth and Fowey in June, but now one month on it was to be home to the 8th Worcestershire Regiment as they helped to build and man the concrete defences against the anticipated German invasion. No cosy barracks, just some old and rather windy Bell tents in clusters amongst ancient oaks and Monterey pines in the parkland of the vast estate. Now this morning he was ordered to take some men and help complete the works at Lostwithiel. He'd never heard of the ancient, little Cornish town nestled in the Fowey river valley, but they'd found it right enough. However, nobody had said anything of an inspection.

"No, captain, this is not that kind of inspection. I have been sent from high authority to ascertain the strengths and weaknesses of our defences in Cornwall. An information gathering mission, if you will, that will help the powers that be make informed choices should Jerry step across the Channel."

The captain shifted uneasily from one foot to the other. He didn't quite know how to broach what he was about to say, and in the end it all just tumbled out.

"With respect, sir, I don't know you from Adam, and I am not about to give a conducted tour of our defences to any stranger who swans up in a Major's uniform. You could be a Nazi spy for all I know. You could have parachuted in as a nun, put on a soldier's uniform and tried to bluff your way into being shown the defences we are preparing." He paused, looking the Major up and down. The Major seemed quite unperturbed by this sudden outburst. The captain continued,

"Besides I don't recognise the regimental insignia on your uniform. And you've no shoulder flashes. I think you better explain yourself."

The Major went to reach a hand down to the large map pocket on his left knee. The captain instinctively put his hand on his pistol in the holster on his belt. The Major sensed his unease and said,

"If I may, captain, I would like to show you a letter that conveys my authority to carry out the task I have been sent back to Cornwall to do."

The captain nodded. The Major carefully unfolded a letter and handed it to the captain who visibly stiffened as he glanced down at it. It was a typewritten letter on headed paper. In the top left of the page was an insignia which incorporated a lion and a unicorn either side of a seal with a crown on top. It was the Coat of Arms of the British Government. His eyes glanced across to the address on the top right "10, Downing Street, Whitehall." The typed date was Monday 1st July 1940. The signature at the bottom was "Winston Churchill". The captain found himself reading it aloud in hushed tones, almost in disbelief.

"To whom has been requested to read this letter, I am writing to instruct you on the authority of the British Government invested in me as Prime Minister that you give your full cooperation to Major Issac Trevennel of Military Intelligence Research MI(R), the bearer of this letter, and immediately furnish him with any information or assistance requested. Major Trevennel is acting on my personal instruction and his mission is of the utmost importance to the defence of this realm in these uncertain days."

The captain's trembling hand gave back the letter. He was somewhat relieved to find the Major smiling. It was the Major who spoke first, his blue eyes sparkling, as he said,

"So I think you'll find I am on your side, captain."

"Yes sir, Captain Mathew Cregoe at your service, sir." The captain saluted.

"Thank you," said the Major. "Not a word of this letter to anyone. Now, how about that conducted tour of your defences you were mentioning?"

"Of course sir, I'd be delighted. If you'd like to come this way," and with a swish of the arm guided the Major towards the Dragon's Teeth. Three lines of the concrete pimples stretched across the road and the verges on either side.

"We have staggered them, sir, to prevent any vehicles getting through."

"But would they stop an enemy Panzer?"

"Hopefully they'd slow him down, sir. We had nothing like this in France. All the positions we had prepared, we were ordered to advance from to meet the Jerry onslaught." The captain hesitated as if he were speaking out of turn.

"Go on, I'm very interested in hearing what you have to say."

"Well, when Jerry hit us we were out in the open, and he was moving so fast we stood little chance. He came at us with tanks and we were trying to stop them with Great War rifles. We lost some good men. If we were in our prepared positions we might have held him a bit longer. It was all rear-guard actions. We retreated 200 miles in ten days to get to Avelin."

"So how could you have stopped Jerry's advance?" The Major's tone was sympathetic. His question wasn't harsh or critical. He seemed genuinely interested.

"I think if we were fighting from prepared positions, then we've got a line to hold on to. The units on your left and right are doing the same. You hold the line. That's why my men have been brought here. Orders of General Ironside, apparently. We are building part of what my superiors call 'The Bodmin Stop Line'. It's to be a line of defences from coast to coast to stop an enemy advance up through Cornwall."

"But will it be strong enough all the way along, or will Jerry sniff out the weak points?"

"I've only been here 24 hours, sir, but from what I'm told there are gun batteries, pillboxes and roadblocks being built along the line. From what I saw in France, sir, if you stop Jerry's tanks, then you stop Jerry. We need strongly defended locations at the places Jerry is most likely to try and punch through the line with his mobile armour."

The Major smiled. He dared not confide in the one expounding the strategy to him, but he knew such an argument was now raging at the highest levels in the British Army. Stop Lines or Anti-Tank Islands and Defended Locations: that was the question vexing the British military strategists in early July 1940. The Great War had been fought in lines and there were those who believed this was the way to secure victory. It had done so in 1918 and surely would again. But the Blitzkrieg in Belgium and France had shown this was a new kind of warfare, a mobile war, and if you denied the enemy the key nodes on the transport system, you would cripple his advance. This was part of his mission from Churchill. As the key protagonists on both sides of the debate tried to win his favour, the Prime Minister had despatched Major Trevennel to see which strategy best fitted the topography of the British landscape. His fellow officer and friend Major Colin Gubbins had been given responsibility in the south east. As Trevennel originated from Cornwall he was put on the sleeper from Paddington, and was told a car would be at his disposal on arrival.

"I suspect we will need a bit of both strategies," Churchill had told the two of them as he explained what he wanted. "I want my own facts," he had said with a twinkle in his eye, "So those army chiefs can't hoodwink me into choosing their pet ideas."

The Major turned to survey the small town, its fourteenth century church spire towering above the clutter of roofs that spread from the hill to the river.

"And I believe Lostwithiel is such a place where Jerry is likely to try to punch through. The river prevents that south of here. This is the lowest crossing point for tanks on the Fowey. So what else have you got to deny Jerry free passage?" he enquired.

"As you can see, sir, the roadblock is just before the bridge over the River Fowey. Apparently this is a new bridge and the road only opened earlier this year. The old bridge is in the town. It's an old Tudor bridge, very narrow and likely to collapse under the weight of a Panzer. My men are preparing charges to blow both old and new bridges if necessary.

"Between the river and the railway, the main line from Paddington to Penzance, we are just camouflaging the pillbox that's been built. Apparently it was constructed by civilian contractors, but they seem to have done a good job. They've followed the specifications and so on. It's been sited so its line of fire covers both the road and the railway line."

"What if Jerry comes up the river?"

"From the quick look I had this morning, the railway embankment south of the town would provide an excellent position from which to fire on any craft coming up the river. However, my men are also constructing a road block at the exit from the

Town Quay into Quay Street. And we are also putting roadblocks up at Downend, up the hill to the east, just in case Jerry tries coming from that direction or up that side of the river."

"Excellent, captain. You're doing well for just a morning here." The Major was genuinely impressed.

"Do you really think Jerry will invade Cornwall, sir?" the Captain said perhaps hoping for some reassurance. "What can he want to come here for?"

"It could be part of a two-pronged attack, south east and south west and meet in the middle before pushing north. It may simply be some diversionary raids to disguise his main assault. He could strike anywhere in the British Isles. He may even use Ireland, in which case Cornwall would be key." The Major spoke with a sense of urgency as if he were trying to stress the importance of the job in hand.

"I suppose he could also strike the cable stations to stop us calling to the Empire and Dominions for help if we were invaded," ventured the captain.

The Major's eyebrow rose slightly at this reference to Britain's undersea cable connections to the Empire and the United States coming ashore at Porthcurno and Sennen. These vital installations added to Cornwall's strategic importance. He surmised,

"If this Captain who's been here a day knows about them, then we can be certain Jerry has a good idea."

"I've got an aunt in South Africa," the captain ventured. "We get a cable greeting every Christmas from Cable & Wireless. So we looked up in a book in the library to trace the route. That's how I know about the cable stations."

The Major was relieved to hear the explanation, though not reassured at the thought of the Nazis wreaking havoc on the Land's End peninsula. He continued,

"So there are many reasons why Jerry may come to Cornwall. We all need to do what we can to be ready. I'm a little surprised he hasn't come already, but come he will. And like in France and Holland and even Poland he'll send his bombers first to soften up the target. If his bombers come to Cornwall, you'll know he intends to invade. How are your men? Are they up to the task?"

"They are fine now, sir," replied the captain. "After Dunkirk, once they'd rested, had some proper sleep and good food, they were fine. We brought our rifles and even some L.M.G.s back with us on the Glen Gower, the paddle-steamer, and although we've had to take on some new recruits back here in Blighty, they're shaping up okay."

"That's good to hear. I understand the Kent Constabulary have been collecting rifles from alongside the railway line out of Dover, so well done to your chaps. Good officers, that's what it is."

The captain smiled. That was the second time the Major had been generous in his praise.

"May I be so bold as to ask a question, sir?" The captain suddenly looked earnest.

"Permission granted," replied the Major. He had warmed to this captain and hoped all he would meet on his mission would be as cheerful and as cooperative as this fellow.

"It's just that some of the men were talking in camp last night with some of the men from the Depot in Bodmin. I guess it's just rumour and tittle tattle, but they were saying there was quite a stir in these parts a fortnight ago. Apparently a dinghy was found up the River Fal with two dead Germans in it."

"Probably airmen whose plane crashed," the Major suggested.

"No, no, spies or agents they reckon. One they think drowned and the other had an injury to his head. Both were dead," countered the captain.

"Well they aren't going to cause any trouble," commented the Major.

"The one with the head injury had had his head bandaged. But when they searched the bodies they found their first aid packages had not been opened. So they think that someone else must have done the bandage. Perhaps a third agent? Tried to save his mate before he died but has then had to leave them? Or maybe a local fifth columnist, you know, a Nazi sympathiser? Any road, they had soldiers out for three days scouring the river banks and woods. They also got those new Local Defence Volunteers involved. It was no small stir from what they told my men. But they never found anyone. It has put the wind up the locals by all accounts. And it's caused rumblings down in Falmouth. The navy wanted to know how a German dinghy got that far up the river!"

"There have been reports of nuns parachuting down all over England," mused the Major.

"But nobody's actually captured a nun," said the captain seriously. "Here they've got two Germans, albeit dead, but there could be a third on the loose."

"So that's why you were so suspicious of me earlier," laughed the Major. "You thought I was your missing Hun. Well, captain," said the Major extending his hand to shake the captain's, "I won't delay you from your vital work any longer. Keep up the good work with your men. It's been good talking to you."

"Thank you, sir. It's been an honour to meet you." The captain smiled and saluted. It was not every day you get given a letter from the Prime Minister to read.

The Major turned to leave then turned back again.

"Oh, I hope they have told you they are getting the LDV to patrol the tunnel on the railway line just about a mile or so upstream from your position. Brownqueen Tunnel, I believe it's called. Just in case any of your chaps run into them, that's what they are supposed to be doing."

The captain opened his mouth to thank him but the words were drowned out by the roar of a motorcycle racing towards them. It was an army dispatch rider, his goggles down over his eyes. The bike was a BSA M20. Officially the colour was known as 'khaki green gas proof No 3'. The men simply called it army green. The rider was in a hurry. He pulled to a halt with a slight sideways skid, cut the engine and propped the machine on its field stand.

"Captain Cregoe, sir. A message from the Depot, sir" he said in the same manner schoolboys recited the nine times table in class. He had taken a folder from the canvas bag slung over his left shoulder and passed it to the captain.

26

Captain Cregoe visibly froze for the second time that afternoon as he read what had been given him. He composed himself with a shake of the head.

"Tell Lieutenant Colonel Comford I am coming straight away. Dismissed, rider." With a salute, the rider turned and mounted the motorcycle. With a hefty kick the engine roared into life and with a twist of the throttle he soon became a blur disappearing back into town. The captain turned to the Major,

"One of my men, a corporal, who was part of the advance party that came down here about ten days ago, has been found dead in his billet. My commanding officer has summoned me back to help investigate."

"Surely that's a job for the police in Bodmin?" said the Major somewhat puzzled.

"Before the balloon went up I was in the Worcestershire Constabulary, C.I.D. branch. Lieutenant Colonel Comford knows my old superior so he drags me into this kind of thing to help out. 'A skilled eye that's loyal to the regiment' was how he put it last time, although that was just some thieving that time. This sounds somewhat more serious."

"I can give you a ride back to Bodmin, if that would help," offered the Major.

"That would be most helpful, sir," said the captain gratefully. "I just need to tell my sergeant I am off. He's quite capable of overseeing what needs finishing off here."

The Major had turned the car round and was sat with the engine running as the captain came striding back down the road from the pillbox.

"This is most generous, sir," said the captain as he climbed into the front seat. The Snipe pulled away.

"Least I can do, especially as I'm going that way. It all seems rather important so good to be able to help out," replied the Major.

"It all seems rather mysterious to me, sir," said the captain. "Comford's note didn't give any details, just an address to report to."

The Major slowed the car, and then turned right up the steep hill towards Bodmin.

"You know your way round these parts then sir?" enquired the captain. He had thought they'd taken the right turn, the way the army truck had brought them this morning, but with all the surprises of the afternoon on his mind, he couldn't be certain. It would make things easier if the Major knew the way.

The Major smiled. "Yes, I am a Cornishman born and bred. My family live further west, but I spent two years at the DCLI Depot in Bodmin before this war started. Well, it was the Munich scare in '38 that got me moved up the line, as it were. My current unit was set up in December of that year, and I was asked to join early in 1939. But enough of that! Anyway, I can find my way round the lanes here."

They passed the school where the caretaker was stood on a ladder taping the windows in a diagonal cross. The Major increased the speed as they left Lostwithiel behind, breaking only for a bend and a junction in the lane.

"So a policeman, eh? Before all this, I mean," said the Major probing.

"Yes I did two years as a constable before my sergeant said I should try out for the CID. I had done three years as a detective before war was declared. I then volunteered. I thought I'd get a better choice if I volunteered than if I waited for them to call me up. Partly because of my previous job, they gave me a commission. And the Worcesters have done all right for me thus far. Though it was a bit hairy getting out of France."

"I was over there for a while. I'd been visiting the French on the Maginot Line when Hun attacked. Came through Belgium and rendered the line totally ineffective. The French Generals couldn't believe that all their energies in the 1930's had been made utterly useless by the same move the Hun made in 1914. You would have thought they would have learned. Enough people told them. They just believed you can't move an army through the Ardennes Forest. How wrong they were. Still they say 'History repeats itself because no one listens!' I moved south through Paris and eventually got a boat at St Nazaire that brought me back to Falmouth."

The Major slowed for the junction at Sweetshouse. It was a small hamlet of several houses and stone barns scattered around the crossroads. A woman was filling a bucket at the pump. There were a few soldiers running barbed wire over some wooden trusses as part of a staggered roadblock. The corporal saluted when he saw the captain sat in the front passenger's seat and waved them through the chicane.

"More of your lot?" enquired the Major.

"Yes sir," replied the captain. "We've orders to build and guard the defences in these parts. That includes the pillbox just there, and the one on the other side of this dip. I can show you the maps back at the Depot if that will help your work."

The road swept past a little chapel and down a hill where a couple of cottages were situated and an entrance to the Lanhydrock Estate. A couple of estate cottages were nestled just inside the gate. As the lane rose up the other side there was another pillbox on the right. It was constructed of concrete block. A couple of soldiers were shovelling earth onto the roof to help disguise it from the air.

"Your men seem to have taken well to the task in hand," commented the Major.

"After the fall of France we all know that Britain's next in Hitler's sights, and I think everyone is rallying to the task, especially now that Churchill is in charge. He seems intent on standing up to the Nazis," replied the captain.

"That he is," agreed the Major. The car slowed again as they passed the vicarage and came to another crossroads. Again there was a roadblock. This one had more of an air of permanence about it and they were asked to produce their papers before being allowed on towards the garrison town of Bodmin.

A tall granite obelisk dominated the skyline as below a steam engine wended its way towards the town.

"What's that monument, sir?" enquired the captain. "I didn't see that from the bus when we arrived last night."

"It's the national monument to Sir Walter Raleigh Gilbert," said the Major recalling the times he'd said that to the men he had made run up to the Beacon and back when he was stationed at the Depot in Bodmin. They'd been allowed a two minute rest at the top to read the inscription.

"Oh, Queen Elizabeth and cloaks over the puddles," said the Captain pleased to be remembering his schoolboy history.

"That's Walter Raleigh," corrected the Major. "Gilbert is a distant relative but he was a Victorian soldier who fought the Sikhs in India. He was twice given a vote of thanks by Parliament and created a baronet by Queen Victoria. His victories in the Sikh Wars were credited with reducing the impact of the Mutiny in that part of India."

"That's some monument," said the captain gazing up at the 144 feet high structure as it appeared again over the trees as they climbed the final hill into Bodmin. "I've seen one like it before at Wellington."

"Yes, by all accounts the Victorians viewed Gilbert as almost as much a hero as Wellington," replied the Major revealing a little of his well-read historical knowledge.

"Now where is it you've got to go? You said the note gave you an address."

"Ah, yes," said the captain, his thoughts being dragged back to the present reality. He rummaged in his pocket for the note from Lieutenant Colonel Comford.

Chapter 3

The two men stood on the pavement gazing at the neat house in St Nicholas Street, Bodmin. It had been easy to find, just a few hundred yards or so further along the road from the barracks, near the railway station. There was a post box in the front wall. It had a small garden in front that seemed to disappear round the side of the property, windows either side of the front door which had a small wooden porch protecting it. The windows to the right of the door were bay windows. Above the windows to the left there was a window for a room in the roof, perhaps the maid's room until not too many years ago. The captain adjusted his cap, and then glanced down again at the paper in his hand.

"Yes, this is it," he said.

"I just don't believe it," replied the Major thumbing through a small notebook. "I am due to contact one of our officers at this address."

When the Captain had told him the address, it had a ring of familiarity about it. Now the Major had checked his list of contacts he knew why. He had merely offered to come in with the Captain out of curiosity, but now he was glad he had. This could prove to be more significant than he had first thought as the motorcycle rider delivered the message twenty minutes ago.

He looked at the captain. He was a clean shaven, brown eyed man with a short stubby nose. He stood at five feet seven inches tall, but had the presence of one used to issuing the orders. Yet the Major had been impressed by the way this officer was hands on with his men in the fulfilment of his orders. As they'd moved around the defences being constructed in Lostwithiel, his men seemed to have a genuine affection and respect for their Captain. Perhaps it was something that had been forged on the roads and fields of Belgium and northern France as the Captain had struggled to extricate his men from the onslaught of the Nazis. Shared experience, especially in adversity, gelled men together in a way that few could understand if they had not been part of that common trial. Captain Cregoe also had an air about him. He was an intelligent man. He knew why he did what he did. Some might call it confidence, others professionalism. Perhaps it was the discipline of his civilian occupation, maybe his military training, perhaps just a depth of character that others would admire. The Major, who was a fairly good judge of men, decided he liked what he saw.

The captain opened the porch door and knocked on the door inside. Its top half was glass with red stained panels decorating it. The door was opened by a small woman in her late forties, possibly early fifties. She was wearing a green summer dress, sandals, and her hair was gathered up at the back. She eyed the uniforms as the Captain introduced himself.

"You'd better be coming in, then," she said with an accent that revealed she wasn't Cornish. "It is a dreadful business. I've never had any trouble here before. He's up in the back bedroom. There are two soldiers up there already."

"I'll take a look and then I'll come and ask you some questions, Ma'am," said the Captain in a manner which showed that this wasn't the first death he had investigated.

The stairs went up on the right hand side of the tiled hallway. There was a large wooden banister. A painting of a Great War aeroplane hung on the wall.

"Ah, Corporal Stainbridge," said the Captain seeing a figure appear at the top of the stairs. The Captain took the stairs two at a time, which showed an athleticism that belied his small frame. The Major followed at a steadier pace. He glanced at the painting. It was a SE5a shown flying over the trenches of the Western Front. The plane was lesser known than the Sopwith Camel but it had shared a major role in gaining the air superiority that was to prove vital in the last year of the war. Its markings showed it to be 84 Squadron of the Royal Flying Corps.

The Major stopped as he stepped inside the bedroom door. He had seen death before. The roads in France had been littered with the bodies of soldiers retreating, old men, women and children, refugees fleeing, the bloated carcasses of their horses and donkeys lying in the ditches amidst their carts and scattered possessions, the victims of Stuka dive bombers dropping their deadly cargo and machine-gunning as they went. Then after a quick glance, he had jolted his mind back to the task in hand determined himself to stay out of the clutches of the Nazi invaders. Now it was different. Here he had come to examine death, to have that conversation with it to see what it would reveal about the one who had perpetrated the crime. In France he had glimpsed the broad brush as he had viewed the casualties of war. Now he was looking for the intricate strokes of the hand that had left its victim. And while he knew every one of those people in France was an individual with a tale to tell, it was the collective story of the collapse of a well-regarded military power that had impacted him then. Here he was face to face with an individual whose story he needed to know and only then would this death's impact be measured.

"This is Corporal Miller," said the Captain who had already begun his task of examining the crime scene. Miller was laid on his back on the bed with his feet reaching the floor. His eyes were wide open frozen in that fixed stare of the departed.

"There is no obvious sign of a wound to his front," the former detective continued, "but given the bruising around his mouth I would suspect…" He paused as he lifted the corpse on to its side. The Major could see a red sticky stain on the bed clothes.

"…and as I thought," the Captain continued, "A stab wound to the back." The Captain looked for a moment or two longer before gently dropping the deadweight back on to the bed. "I suspect he was grabbed over the mouth from behind, to stifle any cry, and stabbed in the back. This looks like our killer knew what he was about."

The Major took this in. "Someone trained in unarmed combat," he thought to himself.

"Stainbridge, anyone else been in contact with the body?" the Captain's attention shifted to his men.

"Not since we've been here, sir. Our orders were to guard the body until you got here, sir."

"What time did you get here?"

"The message to the barracks came in at fourteen fifteen hours, sir, and we were here by fourteen thirty, sir." The captain glanced at his watch. It was now fifteen thirty.

"Who was in the property when you arrived?" he asked.

"Only Mrs Johns, sir. We did a quick search of the house and garden, sir, and I then sent Truscott back to the barracks to confirm to Colonel Comford what we had here, sir."

"Good work Stainbridge. I need you to guard this bedroom a while longer. No one enters without my being here. Is that clear, Corporal?"

"Yes sir," replied Stainbridge saluting.

The Captain paused, gazing around the room, his trained eye looking for any hint that might suggest what had happened he suspected no more than four or five hours ago. There were no obvious signs of struggle. Nothing seemed out of place. Miller's battle dress jacket was on the back of the chair. He glanced at the desk. Nothing was knocked over or looked like it had been dropped suddenly.

"Don't touch the door handle," he said to no one in particular but for everyone's benefit. "Was the door open when you arrived, Stainbridge?" he asked.

"Closed, sir. Mrs Johns opened it for us. She was the last to touch it, sir."

"Thank you, Stainbridge," he said. Then turning to the Major added, "I think we ought to go down and have a word with Mrs Johns."

The Major was relieved. This kind of examination of the dead was not his cup of tea. Questioning people, now he'd had more experience of that. Relieved too, that the body was not that of the officer he was due to visit at this address, but he was also concerned. Was there any link between his man and the body on the bed? No, surely not. There had to be a simple explanation, and he was confident the Captain would find it.

The captain had pencil and notebook in his hand as he spoke. "So, Mrs Johns, when did you discover Corporal Miller?"

"It must have been about ten past two. I'd been down into town, got back about two. He'd asked me to wash some socks for him this morning which I did. When I came back I checked that they were dry on the line. They were, so I took them in and was taking them up to his room. That's when I saw him."

"When did you last see him alive?"

34

"Why, as I said, it was this morning when he asked me to wash his socks."

"And that is something you would usually do?" asked the Captain as he scribbled in his notebook.

"Oh yes, I do what I can to help. You know, all pulling together for the effort."

"Did Corporal Miller give any indication as to what he was going to be doing today?" The Captain looked up awaiting the reply.

"No. No he didn't. No reason to. He comes and goes as he has need to. Apart from breakfast, I don't provide meals here. They get those at the barracks or in town. I let them boil a kettle if they want a drink."

"Why did you send a message to the Barracks rather than phone for the police?"

"It was just as quick to run to the Barracks as it was to go down the Folly and find a telephone. We don't have one here, and neither of the neighbours do," explained Mrs Johns.

"So how many men do you have staying here?" asked the Major, interjecting for the first time.

"Three is the most I can have. My Harry is off in the RAF. That's my husband."

"Ah yes," smiled the Major. "I saw the painting on the stairs."

"He flew planes in the Great War, but they say he's too old this time. He's got a ground job over at St Eval, but I can't tell you any more than that." The Major sensed that was because she was in ignorance rather than being awkward and withholding information.

"So who is staying in the house at the moment?" The Captain brought matters back to the point in hand.

"There is Mister Miller, poor soul. Goodness knows what my Harry will say. Someone murdered in his house while he's away serving King and Country. How will I tell him?"

"I am sure the authorities will do that, Mrs Johns. So Miller is one, who else?" said the Captain with a persistence that belied his gentleness.

"There was the officer, Mr Carlyle. He has the front bedroom over the door. He's been here a couple of weeks but comes and goes. He hasn't slept here every night but where he's staying when he's not here I haven't got a clue. And then there's Johann, he has the back bedroom next to Mr Miller. That's the three. The other bedroom is Harry's & mine, and my daughter uses the attic bedroom."

"And do you know where Carlyle and Johann are now?" asked the Captain.

"No, er, hang on. Mr Carlyle left early this morning saying he wouldn't be back until after the weekend. He did tell me he would be staying in Padstow. Unusual, he never normally tells me where he's going. But Johann must have gone out while I was down the town. I looked round his door when I found Mr Miller but there was no sign of him," replied Mrs Johns.

"What time did you leave for town?" said the Captain as he scribbled in his notebook.

"Must have been just before 11 o'clock," came the reply.

"What time did you last see either Miller or Johann?" asked the Captain.

"This Johann," interrupted the Major. "Is that his surname or his Christian name?"

"His Christian name," said Mrs Johns. "He's Dutch, you see. I couldn't pronounce the surname he told me when he arrived a fortnight ago, so he said it was fine if I just called him Johann."

"Do you have any documents that give his surname?" asked the Major. He raised an eyebrow at the Captain.

"No, he'll have his Identity papers, of course, and as I don't provide meals he keeps his ration book," said Mrs Johns looking a little worried.

"So there's no bacon for breakfast then?" asked the Major.

"No I only provide cereal or porridge. Oh, and I gives them toast if they ask for it, but only with margarine, not butter."

"Coming back to my question, Mrs Johns, what time did you last see Miller and Johann?" asked the Captain a little annoyed at the culinary diversion to his questioning.

"Mr Miller asked at breakfast about doing his washing. He brought it down a little while later. When I hung it out on the line I could see him sat at the table in his room. It looked like he was writing. He had said he wasn't on duty until two."

"And Johann?" the Captain paused in his writing.

"He was at breakfast and then he said he had to go out. I passed him coming back in the hallway as I was going out."

"And that was just before 11 o'clock?" asked the Captain glancing down at his notes.

"Yes."

"What did you do in town, Mrs Johns?" The Captain shifted in his chair.

"I did some shopping. Takes forever these days, the queues you wouldn't believe. Then I looked in at the Royal Hotel. That's where my daughter works but she wasn't to be seen. So I wandered home. Oh, I stopped in the post office to get a stamp so I can write to my Harry. I write every week while he's away. What am I going to tell him about this? He'll be right upset he will," said Mrs Johns, sniffing while her hands were gripping onto the armchair.

"Your daughter, what time did she leave the house?" the Captain had his pencil at the ready again.

"Kara left straight after breakfast. She has to be in work for nine o'clock. She's in charge of the reception desk. She had only been there a few months when the lady in charge left to join the Wrens, so they put her in charge. She's done well for one so young." There was pride in Mrs John's voice.

"How old is your daughter, if I may be permitted to ask the young lady's age?" said the Captain.

"Twenty two."

"Quite a distraction for your guests," commented the Major.

"Oh I'd say. They all seem to be quite sweet on my Kara," smiled Mrs Johns.

"Does your daughter have a young man?" asked the Captain.

"Yes she does, or I should say, she did."

"Oh?" The Captain's eyes fixed on her wondering whether the daughter was involved with the dead soldier lying upstairs.

"She was walking out for a while with one of the Depot lads. Nice chap he was. You know, DCLI," explained Mrs Johns.

"What happened?"

"They had a row, just over a week ago. I heard them on the doorstep. He said 'If she couldn't be faithful to him, then it was better they didn't see each other at all.' 'You don't own me' she replied. 'I will walk out with whoever I choose.' She slammed the front door in his face and stomped up to her room."

"Can you tell me who else she had walked out with?" the Captain probed.

Mrs Johns coloured up as if she'd said too much and was now embarrassed. "I expect it was someone in uniform," she offered.

"But you don't know a name?" the Captain persisted.

"She's not done anything wrong. She's of age, and though I'm sure her father would say a thing or two, he's not here, is he?" she said defensively.

"I'm not saying she has, Mrs Johns," replied the Captain.

"Johann," said the Major deciding it was time to change tack. "When did he first come to stay here?"

"About a fortnight ago. Yes, the 22nd of June, it'll be a fortnight tomorrow."

"You say he's Dutch. How do you know that?" asked the Major.

"That's what he said. He said he had escaped the Nazis and had managed to get a boat from France to England. Said he had arrived in Falmouth. The paper says lots of foreigners came across with our boys." The Captain looked at the Major for confirmation of what Mrs Johns was saying.

"Yes Captain, it was like another Dunkirk. Lots of boats trying to get everyone away. The navy had quite a task trying to sort out who it should load and who it shouldn't. Full to the gunnels most of the ships were. I was one of the lucky ones who made it back. The military were soon put on a train out of Falmouth, though I understood the authorities were processing the refugees at the Princess Pavilion. I guess he's been cleared through," explained the Major.

"Did nothing but sleep and eat for three days when he first arrived. Didn't have much with him, just a case and a bag. But he seems to have money. He paid me a week in advance," said Mrs Johns.

"But why did he come to Bodmin?" asked the Major.

"He said he had secured a job. Didn't say what it was, though. I guess you can't say too much, these days. Careless talk and all those other slogans we see nowadays. He did say to Kara at tea the other night it involved him travelling around on the railways."

"I thought you didn't provide your guests meals, Mrs Johns," interrupted the Major. She went red. The Captain exchanged glances with the Major. Cregoe had missed that one. He was glad the Major was here.

"Well, it was Kara's request. She asked if he could join us," said Mrs Johns sounding a little flustered.

"So is Johann the reason for the falling out with her young man?" enquired the Major.

"Not exactly. I think the row was about Mr Miller. You see he had taken her to the pictures on a couple of evenings." Mrs Johns looked uncertain. She felt these were questions for her daughter, not her.

"So why did she want Johann to join you for tea?" the Major wasn't letting this go.

"Like I said she said, she felt no young man owned her and she could walk out with who she chose. She had gone with Mr Miller when he asked her, but when

Johann arrived I think she rather liked him. Felt sorry for him, a little perhaps, but they seemed to strike it off on the right foot. He speaks very good English, with an accent of course."

The Captain interrupted her, "I will need to speak to your daughter at some point, Mrs Johns, and obviously we will need to speak to Carlyle and Johann as well. My men will stay with you until we have sent along a photographer. He will be from the Military Police. They'll have a look at the scene, check the other rooms. Then we will get the body removed for a post mortem. One of my men will take Miller's personal belongings so that they, in time, can be returned to his family. The Military Policeman will talk to you about informing your husband." The Captain stood up, so the Major joined him. The Captain went upstairs for a quick word with his men. The Major turned to Mrs Johns in the hallway.

"Will you be alright informing your daughter?" he asked genuine concern in his voice.

"I don't know what she'll say, having walked out with him those two evenings. I can see her being mighty upset, but yes, I will be able to tell her. Thank you. She finishes work at six so will be home soon after I expect."

"Thank you Mrs Johns," the Captain said as he stepped off the bottom stair. "You have been most helpful. We will get it all sorted for you as soon as we can."

Their boots crunched on the gravel as they walked back down the path. The Major turned to the Captain.

"So you're satisfied, then?" he asked.

"It seems like the classic love triangle to me. The Military Police can get their teeth into that. I've got rather more pressing things to be concerned with," said the Captain as he adjusted his cap back on his head.

"Is it really that simple?" asked the Major, acknowledging to himself he had no experience of this kind of thing. Reading Bulldog Drummond and Murder on the Orient Express was not exactly the right kind of training for this.

"A jealous young man, a soldier trained in unarmed combat. There's a motive, a method, and all he'd need is an opportunity," said the Captain.

"But why kill Miller if it's Johann who has stolen his young lady's heart?" asked the Major as he walked round the car to the driver's door.

"Perhaps he was unaware of Johann. Going to the picture house is much more public than a cosy tea with your landlady and her daughter. Still, someone else can fathom that one out. I shall tell Colonel Cromford to let the Military Police deal with it. Getting the defences up to scratch is my priority. I assume you are still coming up to the Depot to look at the maps," said the Captain as he eased himself into the passenger seat.

"Certainly, captain. I can give you an hour if you can provide me with a cup of tea. Then I need to track down my man Carlyle." The Major turned the ignition switch and the car roared into life and pulled off up St Nicholas Street. A couple of schoolboys peering through the railings at the station turned to watch as it drove past and up towards the Keep.

Chapter 4

The Major sipped his tea as he sat in Lieutenant-Colonel Comford's office listening to Captain Cregoe explain his conclusions on the afternoon's dramatic events to his superior officer. The Colonel seemed satisfied to accept his Captain's judgement that the matter should be dealt with by the Military Police. A couple of phone calls and the matter was turned over to the Special Investigation Branch of the Corps of Military Police. It was the first serious case for the new officer and his men despatched to Bodmin on their return from France. The Colonel then turned his attention to the Major.

"You are happy with what you have seen of our defences this afternoon," he ventured. Only his facial expression belied the fact that his statement was a question. The Colonel was an older man, in his mid-fifties, with greying hair, a neatly trimmed moustache and an amiable manner. It was he who had suggested Trevennel commence his tour of the defences at Lostwithiel when he had been presented with the Prime Minister's letter early this morning. He hadn't had time to warn his Captain, but felt he would be one who would not let him down.

"Yes, your Captain here seems to have a superb handle on the situation at Lostwithiel, and your men have all been hard at it," replied the Major.

"Good, good. Well, while you've been out and about Jerry has paid us a visit," the Colonel said. "This morning one of his planes shot at a platoon in Charlestown, a little china clay port on the south coast near St Austell, and dropped three High Explosive bombs."

"Grief!" exclaimed the Captain. "Were there any casualties?"

"Nobody killed thankfully," replied the Colonel. "Nine soldiers and a civilian have been slightly wounded. The bombs fell on Major McDougall's residence, on the lawn apparently, but have left the house in a bit of a mess."

"Thank God for that," said the Captain.

"I doubt if Major McDougall is sharing your gratitude," commented the Major with a wry smile.

"No, no, not the house being a mess, the fact that no one was killed," the Captain justified himself. "But I don't recall from studying the maps that this Charlestown place was very big," he continued. "Why would they attack there first? Mind you there are plenty of beaches in St Austell Bay they could land on."

"With several small ports or harbours they could utilise as well. Par, Polkerris, Mevagissey, and even Fowey is not that far along the coast. We'll need to see what Jerry does next to build up a picture of his strategy," said the Major.

"That's not all," the Colonel continued, excited at being the one bearing the news. "Just after two this afternoon a couple of raiders bombed Falmouth Docks. Three steamers were damaged but it seems most of the bombs fell in the water. The chaps working on the Eastern Breakwater had quite a scare apparently as the bombs plopped into the water near them. Again there were only a couple of slight injuries. I had a telephone call from the Castle there just half an hour before you came in."

"Now that's an important target," said the Major. "Falmouth has been designated a Category A port – to be defended at all costs. If they are going to invade Cornwall then they will need Falmouth. It's the third largest natural harbour in the world."

"I hear the defence preparations down there are even more frantic than our own here," said the Colonel.

"They are coming," the Captain said slowly looking at the Major, recalling his comments earlier in the afternoon about bombing raids being a precursor for an invasion.

"I am certain it's a matter of when, not if," replied the Major. "And talking of defence preparations, you were going to show me your maps, Captain. It seems as if we don't have a moment to lose." The two men stood, thanked the Colonel for the tea, saluted and headed for the map room.

A Military Policeman stood by the front door of the house in St Nicholas Street as the Major drove past just over half an hour later. He was on his way to the Bodmin North station to catch an evening train to Padstow where he was hoping to find his man Carlyle. He hadn't revealed to the Captain earlier that Carlyle was on a top secret mission to Cornwall to recruit and set up special groups of men who would go underground and continue the fight against the Germans once they had invaded. He would reprimand Carlyle when he saw him about letting slip where he was going, but he was grateful he had as it would mean less time tracking him down to get an up to date report on how his activities were going. "A gentle word over a meal in the hotel wouldn't be so bad," the Major thought to himself. He was sure he would find Carlyle at Padstow's main hotel, the Metropole, overlooking the station.

The Major turned into Pool Street by the church, drove past the White Hart public house and down to the station. He parked his car to one side of the entrance so it wouldn't be in anyone's way and made his way into the ticket hall.

Having purchased his ticket, the Major turned away from the hatch and then turned back again.

"I say," he began hesitantly. "I don't suppose you have had any foreign travellers come through today?"

"Furriners?" responded the booking clerk from behind the glass. "Yes, we've had a few. This morning there was a couple of Scots lads. They were in uniform, you know, army, like you. Then this afternoon I had trouble understanding a group of blokes. Northumberland Fusiliers was on their shoulder badges. Up north somewhere that is, I believe. They were heading for Falmouth. Goodness knows how they ended up here. Train got diverted, I should think."

The Major was amused. Despite Bodmin being a military town, this railway employee still saw those who spoke with a different accent as foreigners.

"No, no," he laughed. "I mean 'real' foreigners. You know, men who aren't British."

"Now you mention it, yes, there was one. Civilian. Spoke with a… a Dutch accent," said the clerk, his face straining as he struggled to recall. "Well, I'd hazard a guess it was Dutch, not that I've ever been there, but I heard a Dutch man on the radio the other week talking about when the Hun overran their country. Yes, sounded a bit like him." The clerk folded his arms as if he was pleased with himself.

"Can you remember what he looked like?" asked the Major.

"Don't see a lot from in here," came the reply. "He definitely had blond hair. He was wearing a coat. Must have been hot as it's been a warm summer's day. Light brown coat, that's all I can say. Why all the questions?"

The Major ignored the question and posed another of his own. "To where did the Dutchman purchase his ticket?"

"Padstow," replied the clerk looking around for the Station Manager who wouldn't approve of him divulging passenger's information unless it was through the proper channels.

"Thank you, you have been most helpful," said the Major taking the opportunity to let an older gentleman who had come into the booking hall move up to buy his ticket. The Major stepped outside on to the platform.

"Why all the questions indeed?" he thought. "Why all the answers more like? The public are going to have to learn that information is a weapon of war. The amount of information the clerk had divulged in a brief exchange was mind-boggling. Regiments, movements, descriptions. What if I'd been a spy?" The Major chuckled to himself at the incredulity of the notion as he glanced down at his uniform. "Perhaps the clerk had some deference for my rank," he concluded as the sounds of the approaching train echoed up the valley.

The Major climbed aboard the second of the two coaches and shuffled along the corridor until he found an empty compartment. The engine was running round and being watered. Eventually after a quarter of an hour, a shrill whistle indicated they were about to depart. The Major looked at his wrist watch. Right on time, he was impressed. The train pulled out of the station, passed the gasworks and under the bridge next to the old jail. Its walls stood tall and daunting. It was a grim place. The Major consoled himself with the thought it no longer housed prisoners. It had closed and been sold off in the Twenties. As its grey walls disappeared from sight, the Major recalled one of the old Depot men had told him when he was here back in '38 that in the Great War those walls had housed the Crown Jewels and the Domesday Book. A place so secure that the townsfolk believed only one prisoner had ever escaped from it. And he'd got over the wall, but broke his leg in the drop the other side and was easily recaptured. The Major shuddered. Green fields now passed the window as the train made its way down the valley to Dunmere. But thoughts of that grim place would not go away.

The Major pulled an envelope from his inside pocket. He took out the letter and re-read it. He had read it a thousand times before. He stared at the photograph with it, its edges thumbed and worn. He wondered what grim place they might be in now.

"Mind if I take a seat here," said a gentle Cornish voice. The Major looked up with a start. He hadn't even noticed the train had stopped at the little Halt in the cutting at Dunmere, let alone hear the compartment door sliding open.

"Why, of course," he said as he folded the letter and photograph back into the envelope and thrust it back inside his jacket. His new companion, a woman of about forty sat on the seat in the opposite corner of the compartment. She placed her basket on the seat and took out a newspaper. The train pulled away and was soon clickety-clacking its way slowly across the junction at Dunmere, across the River Camel and through the junction at Boscarne before slowing again for Nanstallon Halt.

The Major's mind drifted again to the letter and photograph he had been looking at it. His travelling companion seemed not to want conversation and that suited him. Trees and river became a blur until the train stopped again at Grogley and the woman rose and without saying anything left the train.

The Major could remember little of stopping at Wadebridge or of passing over the level crossing now guarded by troops. It was only the river opening out into the wide expanse of the estuary that brought his thoughts back to the present. The beauty of the view as the train wound its way along the western bank of the Camel never ceased to amaze him.

The train crossed an iron girder bridge. A monument stood on the hill. "What is it with Cornwall and monuments on the hills?" he pondered. This one, he had to confess to himself, he didn't know who or what it commemorated. Now on the final curve into the small port of Padstow he could see the sea beyond the towering cliffs of Stepper Point and The Rumps. Then the train was braking as it pulled into the terminus and he alighted on the platform. His ticket was checked as he left the station. He glanced up and saw his destination up the short slope. The Metropole stood partway up the hill proudly surveying the scene of harbour and station below. The Major straightened his cap and put his best foot forward.

Chapter 5

The Major sat at the breakfast table alone. He dipped the tomato on the end of his fork into the yolk of the fried egg on his plate before savouring the taste. He took in the scene through the window. The sun was already shining on the estuary. The water was a deep blue as the tide was slowly covering the sandbank between the station and the iron bridge in the distance. The gulls were doing a dance as the water on either side ebbed closer and closer. The Major cut the next slice of tomato. He glanced around the hotel dining room. An elderly couple sat at the adjacent table. Across the room by a pillar sat a couple of naval officers. According to Carlyle they were checking out the hotel as the Admiralty were considering requisitioning it for the duration.

The Major thought back to the previous evening. He'd finally tracked Carlyle down, although he wasn't booked into the hotel under that name. They'd enjoyed a fine dinner together. He had delivered the slight reprimand for Carlyle letting slip his whereabouts but he was not too harsh on the poor man as the Major was impressed with how successful he had been in his mission in recruiting suitable men for his Auxiliary Units. Here in the Padstow area he already had the basis for a unit, they had found a suitable location for their hidden hideaway, had constructed it themselves with their own resources, and Carlyle had left early this morning to inspect it and approve it before it was completely re-covered. It was in an old quarry on farmland at Cannalidgey but within easy striking distance of their targets of the railway, the main roads, the port and the aerodromes at St Eval and at Treginegar. Carlyle was pleased. He said he had almost completed his work in this part of Cornwall. He had established Auxiliary Units either side of the Bodmin Stop Line. He had drawn two arcs with his finger either side of the line of the Camel and Fowey valleys and said they would make things unpleasant for any invader trying to move through Cornwall. The Major marvelled at the bravery of such men willing to be recruited for such a task. How long would they survive? But in a desperate fight to repel the invader even a delay of a few hours, or the tying up of men to the rear, could prove to be of vital significance. These were drastic days. The very survival of Britain was at stake, and as her proud history showed, her sons rose to the challenge whenever they were expected to do their duty.

"So I'd better get to mine," the Major thought as he wiped his face with the napkin and drunk the last drop of his cup of tea. "Royal Navy Commander Gordon Campbell, here I come. Let's see how your planned defences of Padstow and the Estuary are coming along."

The Major stood up and was soon leaving the hotel heading for the Headquarters of the Resident Naval Officer. The Major was a little awed knowing he was going to meet a highly decorated veteran of the Great War. He had only discovered that when he had phoned before breakfast to set up his meeting with the Senior Naval Officer and recognised the name having read the Rear-Admiral's account of his wartime exploits on the Mystery Ships or Q-ships as they were known. He was serving in the rank of Commander, but once an admiral, always an admiral. The walk was only a few minutes. He was met by a flag lieutenant and shown to the Admiral's office. He was greeted by the outstretched hand of a stocky fellow in his mid-fifties. He had clear blue eyes, a sailor's weather beaten face, and more medal ribbons than the Major could identify. There was the Victoria Cross, the Distinguished Service Order and two bars, and then a host more the Major was uncertain about, some of them possibly foreign. As he shook the hand the Major noticed the three stripes of a Commander on the sleeve. They looked new on what was a rather worn reefer jacket.

"Welcome to Padstow," said the Commander with a friendly smile. "I'm afraid we've not got a lot for you to see at the moment. It's mostly plans on paper. I have sorted the Navy's plans for the defence of the harbour. Ships, charts, that's my forte. I have requested an army presence, however, to sort the landward defences. I had a phone call from HMS Forte this morning telling me I would be getting a platoon of Northumberland Fusiliers. That's all they could spare from Falmouth apparently. The Fusiliers have to cover the forty miles of coast from Penryn to Praa Sands, so they are pretty stretched. I had to argue that the largest harbour on the north Cornish coast had none. Anyway I'm told a platoon under a Second Lieutenant Dare Wilson will be arriving here on the 10th. So let's hope Jerry doesn't invade before then."

The Major raised his eyebrows. "Let's hope he doesn't come in strength greater than a platoon!" he said.

"It is parachutists and troops attacking from the land that worries me," the Commander said. "The navy will deal with any large force that is coming from the sea."

It seemed to the Major that the irregulars were better prepared than the regulars here in north Cornwall. He glanced round the room. It was fairly sparse. The Admiral was sat behind an old wooden desk in front of the window. A portrait of the King hung over the fireplace, an unopened sherry bottle on the mantelpiece. There was an assortment of charts on the desk in front of the Admiral held in place by a large pebble, a brass paperweight and a hinged ruler.

"You're an army man, Trevennel," said the Commander. "What do you think of pillboxes?"

"As part of a well-prepared position they can be effective for a time," the Major ventured not committing himself totally. "Today's land warfare is much more mobile than the last war."

"I was at a conference yesterday and they seemed to be in vogue. They came up in discussion and everyone was wanting them. So I said Padstow needed some too. Just not too sure of what I've asked for. Falmouth seem to be building a whole line of them to defend the port from the landward side, so I thought they might help here."

"I am sure they could be useful if sited effectively," replied the Major.

"I think that will be a task for this Wilson chap they're sending me. I'll see what he can come up with. He's one of their rising stars, is what I was told. Well, this could be a chance for him to shine. Now let me show you my naval defence. I think Mr Churchill will be impressed, having been First Lord," said the Commander reaching for a chart of the north Cornish coast.

Twenty minutes later the Major was walking in the sunshine down to the small harbour his meeting with the Commander completed.

———————

Twenty four hours on the Major was enjoying a traditional Sunday roast at the hotel. As he cut the tender slices of Cornish lamb into mouth-sized pieces he mulled over the last twenty four hours and what he had learned of the defences in this part of north Cornwall. After his meeting with the Commander yesterday morning he had taken the walk out to Gun Point. It was a delightful walk, only about a mile, but with panoramic views of the Camel estuary. It was a glorious day; both sky and sea were a radiant blue. At St George's Cove some local children were splashing around in the water. It seemed incredulous that his mission was assessing the preparations for war in a place of such beauty and tranquillity. When he arrived at Gun Point there were some of the Commander's men preparing the old Victorian gun mounts and cleaning the steps down to the magazine. Apparently Wilson's Fusiliers would be bringing a couple of six pounder field guns which would defend the estuary while the fixed battery was established. The Commander said the plans were for some 4-inch naval guns to be set up, one even to be placed on the old Barbette Mount from 1780. Whether Wilson would deem them adequate, the Major had his doubts, but any gun was better than no gun. When he had met the Local Defence Volunteers as they assembled for patrol last evening at the Drill Hall in Horsemill Lane a number of them still had broom handles and pitchforks! "How could a nation be so blind as to the forthcoming threat that it found itself in such a defenceless state?" mused the Major as he sliced a roast potato, forked one half of it and put it in his mouth. "Churchill has been warning us for years, but no one listened," he continued. "If we go under, the Appeasers will have a lot to answer for. Still people are beginning to rally to the cry." He wondered if he was just trying to reassure himself. "The people that Carlyle is recruiting show there is some backbone in this country."

The thought of Carlyle jolted him from his musings. Where was he? He hadn't returned to the hotel last night and had not emerged this morning. He had told the Major he would join him for dinner last night but he didn't show. The Major had an uneasy feeling about the situation but he couldn't rationalise why. "I'll give him until teatime," he thought. That seemed a sensible idea. He was due to go with the Commander this afternoon up to the site of the old Great War Royal Naval Air Station at Crugmeer. The Commander was thinking of utilising the site for a naval wireless station Admiralty had requested for this stretch of the coast and he wanted the Major's input as an army man on the practicalities of defending the site. "If there's no sign of Carlyle by the time I'm back I will start making some enquiries," the Major told himself. He glanced up. The waiter was there to remove his plate. He declined the dessert, excused himself from the dining room to ready himself for meeting the Commander.

It was six o'clock when the Major walked into the railway station.

"No sir, no one of that description has bought a ticket from me in the last two days." The booking clerk seemed quite certain.

"Well at least Carlyle has not taken a train to Bodmin," thought the Major as he closed the door behind him. He checked the bus timetable on the board on the wall outside. There was no Sunday service. The last one on Saturday for Bodmin had left at lunchtime, so it was unlikely he had used that form of transport.

"I need to get to the hideout he was inspecting," the Major told himself. "But how? Who would know where it was?" The existence of the Auxiliaries was 'Top Secret' and privy to only a few on a need to know basis. He needed to find a member of the group. He thought back to the LDV group as they assembled last night. One of them has got to be a member. Carlyle had told him he had successfully managed to use the LDV as a cover for some of his groups. It gave them the perfect excuse to be out and about across the countryside at night. "But who in the Padstow group had Carlyle recruited? Come on, think straight. There has got to be a clue," agonised the Major as he strolled towards the harbour. He pictured the group in his mind. One by one he dismissed them; a couple of fishermen, the old captain, a couple of farmers, a shopkeeper – no, can't tell that way. Those holding shotguns, old rifles, a broom handle, a pitchfork, yes, really yes, that's it, got him! The Major stopped with a jolt. He was a foot from the quayside. He was so wrapped up in his own thoughts he was oblivious to what he had passed and to where he was heading. The realisation had come to him just in time or he would have pitched headlong into the water.

The Major could see him now. A slimly built man, probably just turned forty. Blue eyes, clean shaven, short back and sides. He was one of the few to carry a Lee

Enfield .303 rifle, but that was not it. The Major had only caught a quick glimpse as the man had obviously sought to hide its holster under the coat he was wearing. But now it was as clear as day. The pistol. This was no old duelling pistol taken from above the fireplace resurrected to service once again in time of national desperation, this was a 400 Colt .32in semi-automatic. The Major believed it to be an American weapon, often used by their police where in the major cities like New York the policemen were usually armed. He had seen them in photographs in a magazine article. The Major knew from his friend Gubbins that the Prime Minister had made the Auxiliary Units a priority for revolvers. He knew his man; now to find a name and then to locate him.

The LDV had begun to assemble yesterday evening from half past six. The Major hoped they would again tonight. He would go along and see if he could find his man. He made his way through Padstow's narrow streets up the hill to the Drill Hall.

The Major, warmed by the brisk climb, was a little rosy cheeked as he turned the final corner. The caretaker was just coming out having opened up the hall for the LDV. The Major nodded to him as they passed, and he let himself into the hall. Only the corporal was there moving chairs at the far end. He hadn't noticed the Major's arrival.

"Good evening," said the Major making the man start. "I wonder if you can help me." The Major described the physical appearance of the man he wanted without mentioning the pistol. "He was here last night when you assembled for patrol. I would like a word with him and thought he may be back this evening."

"You won't find Mr Treluckey here on a Sunday night," said the corporal once they'd established just who the Major was looking for.

"Do you know where he might be, or where his home is?" enquired the Major.

"He'll be at the Gospel Meeting," said the corporal picking up another chair.

"What's that? Or perhaps, more to the point, where's it held, this Meeting?" the Major asked trying not to sound impatient.

The corporal looked incredulous. "Why, it'll be in the Gospel Hall," he said.

"You'll have to give me a few more details," said the Major wondering what kind of event and place this might prove to be.

"Mr Treluckey is a devout man of faith and will be attending the meetings at the Gospel Hall on a Sunday. 'Nothing comes between him and his Lord' he told the captain when he signed up in the LDV."

The Major teased some directions out of the corporal, clarified by another of the volunteers who had just arrived, and set off down a steep path back into the town. He soon found himself in Barry's Lane and was then climbing the other side of the valley. He made his way into High Street and just a few doors along he was stood in front of a noticeboard that declared this building tucked amongst the terrace of cottages and houses was the Gospel Hall. It didn't look much like a church, but it was clean and tidy. The woodwork had been recently painted. The noticeboard was blue with gold lettering. It announced there were a regular Sunday morning service and a Gospel Meeting at 6:30pm. He glanced at his watch. It was now 7:25pm. The door was ajar and the Major stepped inside into a small porch. A shelf in front of him was stacked with hymnbooks and a few Bibles. There was another door to the side and the Major gently opened it and went in.

Now the Major thought he had entered quietly so as not to disturb anything that might have been happening inside, and indeed, he had. However, it seemed as if the man speaking at the front paused, and about thirty pairs of eyes turned to peer at the one who had come to the service just as it was about to end. The Major eased himself uncomfortably into a seat in the back row. The man at the front resumed by announcing the number of the closing hymn and the congregation turned back to find their hymnbooks. A man sang the first line, a bit like a cantor in the synagogue the Major thought, and then the congregation stood and joined in with a relish and a fervency he had never heard before. He stood. It seemed the right thing to do. Everyone else was. A lady in the row in front turned and gave him her hymnbook.

"Will your anchor hold in the storms of life,
When the clouds unfurl their wings of strife,
When the strong tides lift and the cables strain,
Will your anchor lift or firm remain?"

The Major looked around the hall. Above the man at the front a Bible text was painted in a banner on the otherwise plain white wall. There was no altar, just a wooden table with a white lace cloth and a vase of freshly picked flowers. The chairs were all in rows facing the front. The row in front of him seemed to be a group of four ladies of varying ages. In front of them a couple of matlos were singing away heartily. "Well, the song does seem to have a naval theme," thought the Major. In front were a family: mother, two small children, then father. Another older couple sat in front of them. At the front sat a couple of young lads, perhaps about fourteen or fifteen. On the other side of the aisle was a similar array of families and older couples. In the back row opposite him was a woman in her forties, a young woman in her early twenties and a young boy aged about nine. The boy at the end of line would steal a glance at the Major until the young woman noticed and nudged him with her elbow. The boy looked up at her, she frowned. The boy turned back, looked at the Major and raised his eyebrows as if saying "Big sister caught me again!" The Major gave a faint smile. The congregation were now letting forth in the chorus for the final time.

"We have an anchor that keeps the soul,
Steadfast and sure while the billows roll,
Fastened to the rock which cannot move,
Grounded firm and deep in the Saviour's love."

The Major's eyes dropped to the book. The words were credited to a Priscilla Owens (1829-1899). He closed the book and returned it to the lady in front of him. The man in front was now praying, but he wasn't reading anything. This was an extemporaneous prayer. He spoke passionately and fervently rising to fever pitch as he intoned the Almighty on behalf of Bobby, a Scots missionary who had recently arrived at the Camundambala Mission in the Portuguese colony of Angola, until the last sentence when the volume and intensity dropped off to a final "Amen" which was echoed by the congregation.

Everybody then sat down. The Major did likewise. It didn't look as if his man was here. There was an eerie silence for about twenty seconds and then several conversations all started at once. Several of the ladies in the row in front of the Major turned and greeted him saying it was nice to see him. One of the men from a couple of rows forward came back and shook his hand. The Major seized his opportunity.

"I am looking for a Mr Treluckey," he ventured, "and I was told I would find him here on a Sunday."

"You were told correctly," came the reply but the Major sensed there was more to come. "However, this evening he has driven to Newquay to take the Gospel Meeting at the assembly there."

"Oh," said the Major trying to disguise his disappointment. "I was hoping to see him rather urgently."

"His family are here," replied the man. "Maybe they can help you and pass a message or something." He turned across the aisle. "Hannah," he said. The older of the two women squeezed along the row. "This gentleman," he began. He turned back to the Major. "I'm sorry I don't know your name."

"Major Trevennel."

"Major Trevennel is looking for your husband. I told him he had gone to Newquay to preach, but maybe you can be of assistance to him." The man eased aside.

"Well, I'm guessing by the uniform, Major, that it is military matters you wish to speak with my husband about."

"My father was in the Great War," piped up a young voice. The young boy was at his mother's elbow, a glow of pride across his face.

"Hush, David," said his mother. "My husband won't be back until about nine o'clock this evening."

"Arr, I do rather need to see him tonight," said the Major.

"You are welcome to come home and wait if it's that urgent. I can put the kettle on and make you a cup of tea until he gets back."

The Major looked at Hannah. She was dressed smartly in a blouse and jacket with a matching skirt. She had shoulder length hair with a summer hat perched on top. She was about five feet two, five feet three in height. She had a slender jaw, but her eyes were warm and friendly.

"That would be most kind," the Major replied.

"The soldier's coming to our house," the young boy had turned to the young woman who was still sat in the row opposite.

"You are welcome," said Hannah. "There's just one small problem. We live on a lane about a mile or so out of Padstow, and as my husband has the car, we will have to walk."

"That's perfectly okay," said the Major regretting leaving his car in Bodmin. "At least it is a pleasant summer's evening."

Chapter 6

After the family had said some farewells to a few of the congregation, they stepped outside with the Major, leaving an excited buzz of curious gossip in the hall. The Major fell into step with Mrs Treluckey with her daughter and son following behind. The Major found himself retracing his steps across the valley and up the path that came out on the lane near the Drill Hall. They continued up the hill past the Drill Hall, past the school and on into the country. The Major learned from Mrs Treluckey that her husband was only an occasional preacher. He had had no formal training but people seemed to enjoy what he had to say. He had seen service on the Western Front in the last year of the war. Some of his training had been done down at Falmouth which is where she had met him. Apparently there were some trench systems dug in the woods below Pendennis Castle and these had been used to train the troops. They had met while out promenading along the seafront on a Sunday evening. He had managed to survive the conflict unscarred physically, although he refused to talk about it much saying he had seen things no young man should ever have had to witness. He came back to Falmouth after the war, where they married and where their daughter was born the same year. They moved to Padstow when an aunt died and left them her small farm with its cottage. That's where David was born. It had been rather run down when they moved in but Mr Treluckey had worked hard to make the farm a success and things were much more comfortable now. They had just passed the end of Sarah's Lane when the life history was interrupted.

"We take the path over the fields here," Mrs Treluckey said, pausing by a stone stile. "It saves about a mile if you follow the lanes around, and this time of year it isn't muddy."

The Major climbed the stile first and then stood on the far side offering a hand to the ladies as they looked for the small granite steps protruding from the hedge. Mrs Treluckey nimbly descended, having taken the proffered assistance, and said "Thank you." Her daughter, now with her hat in hand, made her own way down, but on the second step slipped and lunged forward. The Major caught her with both arms and gently stood her back on her own two feet.

"That was rather clumsy of me," she said going slightly red. "Thank you awfully for catching me."

"Happy to be of service, Miss …" the Major's voice trailed off as he realised he didn't know her name.

"Elizabeth," replied the young woman finishing his sentence.

"That's a pretty name," said the Major noticing for the first time just how pretty its bearer was. Elizabeth had long flowing blonde hair that he hadn't seen before as it had been hitched up at the back allowing her Sunday hat to perch comfortably on her head. She had a face that would grace a Hollywood movie. She smiled at his comment with deep blue eyes. She had a slender figure, a pert bosom, long legs, but it was the eyes that drew the Major's attention. He fell in beside her as they walked, not quite knowing how to further the conversation. Up ahead young David could be heard telling his mother "She fell on purpose, she did. I could tell." Hannah shushed her son's nonsense conscious the Major and her daughter were only a few yards behind.

"I'm Isaac," said the Major introducing himself.

"Isaac, the one who laughs," commented Elizabeth. "Then I shall call you Zac." The Major gave a wane smile. His mother had never liked shortened names, but he didn't want to make an unfavourable impression so he bit his tongue.

"So do you work or are you a lady of leisure?" the Major eventually asked awkwardly. Elizabeth laughed.

"My father's farm does well, but he's not rich enough to be able to keep me. I'm not a Prideaux," she said doing a twirl as she walked.

"I assume the Prideaux family are some local gentry," the Major enquired.

"Yes they live in the large house on the hill back over there," said Elizabeth turning to point. "You can just see the top of Prideaux Place from here." The Major looked but wasn't too sure what he was looking at. The skyline seemed to be all hedges and trees. He was glad when Elizabeth turned and started walking again. She continued, "No, I had a job in the Post Office here in Padstow, but four weeks ago I signed up for the ATS. I'm still training at the Depot at Bodmin. This weekend was the first leave we were given so I came back home. I go back on the train in the morning."

"What does your father think of having a daughter in the army?" The Major was curious. He had judged this to be quite a traditional family, and given Hannah's comments about her husband's service in the Great War, it wasn't quite what he was expecting.

"He's rather proud, I believe. We were listening to the wireless during the evacuation of Dunkirk, and he was moaning that the soldiers had been sent to France to do a new war job with old war weapons, and saying perhaps now people would realise that it will take a united effort to stand up to Hitler with everyone in the country doing their part from the men in the factories, the farmers in the fields to the soldiers and sailors and airmen. So the next day when I came home and told him I had signed up, he said "I'm sorry it's come to this lass, but I'm proud of you for being determined to do your bit." It's mother who's not so sure. With me away and Dad busy with his LDV, she's had to do quite a bit on the farm. My father said to me this weekend he would try and get someone in to help with the milking. That will ease some of the burden on mother."

They had come to another stile. "Will you let me help you this time?" the Major said smiling.

"As I know you have big strong arms to save me, I just might," Elizabeth teased. They made it over without mishap, but the Major did notice a ring on Elizabeth's left hand. He was surprised he felt disappointed. He tried not to let it show.

"These are our fields now," Elizabeth explained. "That's Churchey Cottage you can see up there," she said pointing up a path off to the right, "And we are just a little bit further at Trerethern, off over to the left."

The small cluster of buildings soon came into view, nestled in a valley that ran down to a creek. The Major was intrigued by this family. Father was a Great War veteran who had been recruited into the Auxiliaries, though the Major was aware his family would be oblivious of this. They simply thought he was busy with the LDV. He was also a man of faith given his preaching engagement this evening. Mother came across as a confident, well organised kind of woman. Daughter, not only got her good looks from her mother, but shared that air of confidence. And the son, well, he was just a nine year old boy.

David stood holding the final gate open for them, and then swung on it as he shut it behind them. "There's the motor launch again," he said excitedly waving an arm around furiously. From the gateway the view down across the Camel estuary was breath-taking on this summer's evening. There churning up the water behind it was a grey naval motor launch making its way down the river towards Padstow.

"She's a beaut," said the Major returning to the gate where the young boy stood on the rungs to see over the stone wall. "HDML – harbour defence motor launch."

"How fast can it go?" said the enquiring young admirer.

"I think it's got a top speed of about 12 knots," said the Major wondering whether he was revealing any military secrets.

David was still telling the Major about the first time he had seen the launch a few days ago as Mrs Treluckey directed them into the front room of the small farmhouse and disappeared out again to put the kettle on. Elizabeth had vanished upstairs, so the Major was left with the young lad.

"What do you want to be when you grow up?" asked the Major thinking he might have a young sailor on his hands.

"Why, mister, have you run out of ideas?" came the unexpected reply.

"No, I, er," the Major spluttered, somewhat amused at this display of boyish humour.

"David!" exclaimed his mother returning to the room. "We will have less of your cheek, thank you very much."

"I am going to be a Spitfire pilot when I grow up," David ventured. "I saw some earlier taking off from St Eval and heading south over the hills."

"Now that's an ambition I admire," said the Major looking up as Elizabeth returned to the company. She had brushed her hair and was looking quite stunning.

"His ambitions change every week depending on which bit of excitement he's just seen," said Elizabeth dismissively.

"Leave him be," Hannah cautioned, having come to stand in the doorway. "Without a vision the people perish so let the boy dream. Now I can hear the kettle whistling. Please excuse me while I make the tea."

"I love him really," said Elizabeth putting a big sisterly arm around David's shoulders making him blush. She turned to the Major. "Do you have any family?"

"No, I'm not married. But I do have a brother. He's a couple of years older than me. He married and they have a son." The Major's expression became more serious as he thought of the family he had not seen for several years. Elizabeth sensed she may be treading on sensitive ground.

"I'm sorry if I've asked the wrong question," she said gently.

"No, it's quite alright. I haven't seen my brother or his family for a while."

Elizabeth didn't know what to say so there was a silent pause before the Major added, "They lived in Austria. The last anyone heard of them was in February last year, and now with the war, it has made communication well-nigh impossible."

"I'm sorry. I hope you hear soon," said Elizabeth glad her mother returned at that moment with a tray of tea. She stirred the pot, let it brew a while and then poured them all a cup of tea, adding the necessary quantities of milk and sugar, and offered round slices of homemade fruit cake. The Major took in the homely scene wondering just what impact the war would have on homes like this, and praying it would not be like that of his brother's on the continent. Hannah's cheerful chatter as host, along with a second slice of cake, helped the Major to relax. When she was clearing up their plates, cups and saucers the Major noticed a photograph of a young sailor on the sideboard.

"Which relative is in the Navy?" he asked. Mrs Treluckey paused and glanced at Elizabeth. She had gone white and was looking at the floor. No one spoke.

"Now I've asked the wrong question," the Major said sensing the awkwardness his enquiry had caused.

Elizabeth swallowed hard. "He was my fiancé," she began, her voice cracking with the emotion. "He was lost on the Royal Oak when she was sunk last October."

"I'm so sorry," said the Major. Hannah disappeared to the kitchen with her tray. Elizabeth seemed to find some courage from somewhere to continue. "That's the other reason why dad didn't say anything when I joined the ATS. He knew I wanted to help defeat the evil that had caused such loss."

Now it was the Major's turn not to know what to say. He knew the Royal Oak had been sunk in Scapa Flow by a submarine that had penetrated the defences, but knew he couldn't discuss military details. He just nodded. Hannah popped her head round the door. "I hear a car in the lane. I think it must be your father returning." David leapt up to follow his mother to the front door.

The Major turned to Elizabeth, "I think you are a remarkable young woman. Your family and your country will be proud of you."

She looked at him, her deep blue eyes moist. "God gives me the strength to do what needs to be done. But thank you."

At that moment Mr Treluckey stepped into the room and held out a hand to the Major who stood up to shake it. Introductions were made and once Hannah had supplied her husband with a cup of tea, the family withdrew leaving the two men to talk. The Major outlined his concern for Carlyle and made his request. Mr Treluckey listened intently, his face betraying no emotion. His reply took the Major aback.

"I am sorry, sir, I know nothing of this man or this group of whom you speak."

"The pistol," said the Major and went on to explain his view of its significance.

"I am a member of the LDV and we are supplied with whatever weapons are available. I accept that is an odd assortment, and as yet we have more men than rifles or guns."

The Major realised he wasn't penetrating the cloak of secrecy. He was impressed, but he had one trump card up his sleeve, or rather, in his jacket inside pocket, and he reached for it, and gave it to Mr Treluckey without comment. He took it, read it, glanced at the reverse and handed it back.

"The family don't know or suspect a thing," was all he said. He got up and went out into the hallway. "Hannah, dear," he called, "I've just got to take the Major onto his next Volunteers unit. I'm not sure how long I'll be. Don't wait up if I'm not back by bedtime."

He returned and nodded for the Major to follow. Nothing more was said until they were driving up the rough farm lane.

"So it was the pistol that gave me away?" asked Mr Treluckey.

"Only because I was aware that groups like yours have priority on the supply of revolvers. It wouldn't stand out for anyone else."

"We've only been formed a fortnight. One of the first groups recruited I'm told. We only finished building our hideaway this past week. Lieutenant Carlyle was coming to inspect it on the weekend before we finally seal it until it's needed. I haven't heard how that went, having been busy with the farm on Saturday and with the assembly today."

"Carlyle was staying at the same place as me, but failed to return yesterday evening. He hasn't shown through the day today. That's why I'm somewhat concerned." The Major said nothing of events in Bodmin.

The farmer was driving through the narrow Cornish lanes at what the Major considered to be breakneck speed. They barely reached thirty but the hedges were high and the Major didn't have a clue where he was being taken. At a couple of junctions there was the post of the signpost but the arms had been removed to deny any help to the invader. The Major wondered what hindrance that might prove to the defender, especially as regiments from counties far away across the Tamar were now in Cornwall to protect it. Then the farmer slowed as they came down a short hill, and pulled the car off the lane against a small rock face.

"We walk from here," was the only direction given. They went through a gate, crossed a field that sloped steeply up to the left. A small stream gurgled its way through the undergrowth off to the right. They went through another gate and came into a small quarry that obviously had not been worked for some years. They crossed the quarry and started on a track that climbed the hill that rose in front of them. Mr Treluckey suddenly stopped and froze.

"The trap door is open," he said in the faintest of whispers. The Major looked all around him. He could see no kind of entrance. The farmer moved quietly through the gorse to his left and then crouched down. The Major followed and now he saw in the ground before him a small square opening.

"No member of the group would leave it like this," whispered Mr Treluckey. The Major pulled out his pistol, but the farmer was already climbing down on the rungs inside the opening. He went down about three or four feet and then crouched down and disappeared from view. The Major peered down into the darkness and decided he'd better follow. "A torch would be more use than a pistol right now," he thought. His feet felt five rungs down and then he stepped onto the ground. He turned and a tunnel about two feet across, two and a half feet high disappeared from the shaft. He was clambering his way along when a torch was suddenly switched on ahead of him. After sixteen yards that seemed much longer to the Major, he emerged into an underground room. There stood the farmer, torch in hand. The Major straightened himself up and found he could stand. He gazed around following the beam of the torch as the farmer checked the hideout. The walls were made of concrete block. The roof had what looked like rails from the railway placed regularly along its length with timber filling the gaps. There was obviously concrete on top of that as some had seeped through a crack in the timber just above their heads. To the right of the entrance there was a shelf in the wall that was stacked with an assortment of tins and containers. There was a small stove with a chimney going through the roof in one corner. Two wooden bunks stood against the far wall. On the same wall as the entrance there was a sliding door. Mr Treluckey pushed at it. It seemed stiff. He gave it more of a heave and it ran along its runners. At waist height there was another tunnel. As the farmer shone his light onto the tunnel the Major caught sight of a foot. He stepped closer.

"Here's your man," said Mr Treluckey. The body was lying face down motionless.

"Let's lift him out here where we've got more room to see," said the Major. The two men struggled to lift the officer out of the tunnel and half placed, half dropped him onto the floor. The Major could see there was a wound to the back. There was a large sticky red stain on his coat. He rolled Carlyle over. There was nothing to be done for him. He had been dead a fair while. He did notice there was some bruising about the mouth. Immediately he thought back to Captain Cregoe's examination of Miller.

"I believe this is not the first time this killer has struck," said the Major. "I need to get to a telephone where I can talk freely. You need to check on all the other members of your patrol and to make sure they are alright. This could constitute a serious breach of your secrecy if the killer is not caught quickly."

"The brothers' farmhouse is not too far. They are in the patrol and you will be able to phone from there. What do we do with him?"

"Leave him. I'll arrange someone to come and collect him. We need to move quickly. I suspect the killer has got a day on us and that could mean trouble anywhere."

Without a word they made their way out of the tunnel. The farmer shut the trap door and disguised its presence. It wasn't until they were in the car that he spoke.

"Who do you think the killer could be?"

"I am beginning to think we have a Fifth Columnist or an enemy agent at work. This is the second military death within as many days. The first was at Carlyle's lodgings in Bodmin. I'm not sure if the two are connected, but Carlyle's role in the setting up of the Auxiliary Groups makes tracing his killer of the utmost importance."

"Nothing seemed to be disturbed in the hideout. The food was untouched. And there's no papers left there that would compromise the group. The lieutenant's killer may not have realised the significance of the location."

"Let's hope so," said the Major. "Who from your group was taking Carlyle to the hideout?"

"That would have been the Sergeant," said the farmer. "You don't think he…" His voice trailed away as the enormity of what he was about to ask hit him.

"We can't rule anything out," said the Major with a growing sense of doom. The farmer turned left at a T junction. He drove on for about half a mile and pulled off into a small yard. In front of them stood a typical Cornish farmhouse, its upper walls slung with slate as additional protection against the south-westerly gales. One of the brothers answered and ushered them into the kitchen. A brief explanation was given and use of the phone on a dresser against the kitchen wall was offered.

"You first," said the Major to Mr Treluckey. "We need to know the rest of the patrol are safe, including the sergeant."

"The Sergeant's fine," said their host. "He came over yesterday evening with the news the hideout had passed inspection, and to arrange for us to meet on Monday morning to finish covering it with soil and rocks from the quarry. He was mighty pleased. 'A good piece of work' he said Carlyle had called it. He said the inspection was all over in less than an hour."

Mr Treluckey picked up the phone and spoke to the operator. The Major scratched his head. "Was the Sergeant implicated? If so, how had the Fifth Column been able to penetrate this new secret group? If not, when and why did Carlyle return to the hideout? Questions, questions, questions and no answers. What was he to do? He would phone Captain Cregoe at Bodmin and get him to come and examine the body and see what clues he could find. He would have to report Carlyle's death to London. The loss of an Intelligence Officer so soon in the operation was a serious blow. Was this connected to the death in Bodmin? If so, how?"

Mr Treluckey interrupted his train of thought. "The Sergeant is safe and well. He says he left Carlyle at the crossroads in St Issey just after ten o'clock yesterday morning both pleased that the hideout was up to scratch. He was shocked at the turn of events and said he'd come over to offer what assistance he could. I'll telephone the others." He lifted the phone again and waited for the operator to speak.

The Major tried to put himself in Carlyle's shoes. "If I considered the inspection successful, why would I return to the hideout? Would I try and find it by myself? Wouldn't that test whether the tunnel entrance could easily be found, or stumbled upon? But why would the killer meet him there? Or had he been followed? Was Carlyle just an unfortunate victim or was he targeted? Is the killer of military significance? The Captain had called the murder in Bodmin a love triangle. Was this connected? Was it the same killer?"

He was still wrestling with the questions when Mr Treluckey reported that all of the patrol were safe and well. At least it seemed to the Major that it was Carlyle that was targeted rather than the group.

He made his phone calls. Captain Cregoe was coming out straight away and would bring the Military Police officer with him who was now handling the Bodmin death. Cregoe felt he could be trusted. London wanted to send a man to investigate, but would wait on an update from Major Trevennel tomorrow lunchtime before putting him on the train at Paddington. They would start the search for a suitable replacement for Carlyle straight away.

The Major and Mr Treluckey accepted the offer of a cup of tea from the farmer in whose kitchen they had made themselves at home. The Sergeant arrived shortly afterwards and confirmed his story of the meeting with Carlyle, and dropping him off in the village. He had no knowledge of Carlyle's intentions or planned movements, and was surprised as any of them at his return to the hideout. The more he spoke the more the Major sensed Carlyle's killer didn't come from within the group of men the deceased officer had hand-picked for their secret resistance role. It took a full hour and a half for Captain Cregoe to arrive from Bodmin on a Military Police motorcycle with sidecar. They had had to stop several times to consult their map by torchlight at the numerous unfamiliar junctions in the windy lanes of this part of north Cornwall. It was quite a little party that trudged through the field to the quarry to the hideout.

Less than an hour later Cregoe had confirmed the Major's suspicions that this was probably the work of the same hand that had struck in Bodmin. There were too many similarities and the connection seemed too strong for them to think otherwise. Unceremoniously they had dragged the body out of the hideout and had placed it in the sidecar of the combination. "We can't leave it where it is. The fewer people who know this location the better," the Major had said. The farmer was all for digging a grave in his nearby field, but Cregoe said it would be better if they took the body back to the Barracks and got the contract undertaker to deal with things from there. The Sergeant had secured the hideout and he and the farmer said they'd walk back up the lane to the farm. The Military Policeman kicked the motorcycle into life, Cregoe climbed onto the seat behind him, and with a hat over Carlyle in the sidecar, they disappeared up the lane in the opposite direction and turned towards St Issey. The Major turned to Mr Treluckey and asked "Could you be so kind as to drop me back to my hotel in Padstow?"

"You can't go back looking like that!" The reply surprised the Major who had not noticed the dirt on his dishevelled uniform, let alone the blood on his hands from when they had moved the corpse and across his face where he'd wiped his hand across it. "You'd better come back to the cottage and clean up. You can sleep with us and I'll drop you in in the morning. I'm sure that will avoid the questions if you turn up at this hour looking like I don't know what."

The Major looked at his watch and was staggered to see it was just past one in the morning. He accepted Mr Treluckey's kind offer and eased himself into the passenger seat. Fifteen minutes later they were bumping down the lane to the farm.

Chapter 7

The Major woke with a start. Sunlight was streaming through a chink in the curtains. Someone had already been in and removed the blackout. He wondered where he was and why he was sleeping on the floor. This wasn't his hotel room. Then it all came back to him. He got up quickly and stretched. He was at full stretch in just his vest and pants when the door opened behind him and Elizabeth's voice said, "Oh I'm so sorry, I didn't realise…"

The Major turned to see her head disappear out of sight while a hand on the door held it just ajar. He pulled on his trousers and buttoned them up.

"I'm tickety-boo now. I think your eyes will cope with the sight that greets them," the Major said amused at her embarrassment, but not quite sure whether he should be embarrassed himself.

The head reappeared. "I'm awfully sorry. Mother sent me to collect our guest from the front room for breakfast. She didn't warn me the guest had been sleeping here."

"I'll just put my shirt on and then I'll follow you right along," the Major smiled.

The family were all seated at the table when the Major found his way to the large farmhouse kitchen. As he sat down Mrs Treluckey put a plate of eggs and bacon in front of him. He breathed in deeply through his nostrils making his hosts believe he was soaking in the aroma and picked up his knife and fork. Bacon! How was he to get out of this one? He was just about to attack his eggs with relish when he felt a sharp kick on his shin under the table. He looked around startled and saw Elizabeth looking at him intently shaking her head as if to warn him not to start. He replaced his knife and fork. After Mrs Treluckey had served the rest of the family she sat down and they all bowed their heads. Somewhat bemused the Major did the same but glanced across at Elizabeth for some clue as to what was going on. She winked at him as her father began to say grace.

"Father, we thank Thee for Thy blessings this day and may this food give us strength to do Thy will. In Jesus' name, Amen."

The Major had not been part of such a scene since his grandfather used to intone a blessing on family meals when he was a small boy. It brought childhood memories flooding back to him: of visits to his grandparents' home in Penzance; of the large candelabra his grandmother would light; of rituals done in their home as the synagogues in Penzance and Falmouth had closed years before as numbers dwindled; of going with his grandfather to the synagogue in Penzance tucked up an alley off New Street which had been sold and become, that's where he'd come across them before, a Gospel Hall. The Major smiled to himself at the connection. He could picture his grandfather putting his hand on the lintel and saying a prayer. One afternoon they were surprised by a lady coming out. She had been doing some cleaning but let them in for a look. Grandfather was relieved to see the Ark was still there on the far wall and even the two Decalogue tablets above it were in place. He could remember climbing up to the Ladies' Gallery to look down at the chairs below set out around a central table. Perhaps that's why he felt such an affinity with this family. Not that either his parents or himself had been one for ritual and faith. He remembered walking with his grandfather shortly before he became ill and died. They had strolled along the Promenade at Penzance and his grandfather had gently chastised him for letting his faith slip.

"You mustn't do that!" The Major was sharply brought back to present reality. He glanced around the family at the table and was relieved the comment was directed at young David playing with his bacon rind. His grandfather would turn in his grave if he could see the Major, his favourite grandson, being given eggs and bacon. How things had slipped in just two generations. But then army life wasn't geared up for those of different religions. Certainly the officers he knew were all Anglicans, nominally at least, and while there were Catholic and Methodist padres, the established church was taken as the norm. He'd just gone with the flow. It wasn't something that mattered to him. It wasn't something he had given a lot of thought to until the last twenty four hours, well, until he'd come into contact with this family. They hadn't said anything, certainly hadn't discussed religion, but he had found himself asking himself questions about them and reflecting on his own background.

A knock came at the door. Mr Treluckey went to answer it. Apparently it was a neighbour asking for some milk and when Mrs Treluckey rose from the table to deal with it and Elizabeth went to the door to answer the neighbours enquiries about her

71

in person the Major used the distraction to ask young David if he fancied some extra bacon. He nodded enthusiastically and the Major slipped the two rashers off his plate and on to the lad's with a look that said to say nothing. The boy smiled and the Major sensed he'd just made a friend for life. Elizabeth was the first to return but she hadn't twigged what had gone on.

When the farmer and his wife returned to the table much of the conversation was about the tasks on the farm, but as the plates were emptied it now turned back to the Major.

"How long are you staying in Padstow?" asked Elizabeth. He gave a non-committal reply.

"Do you ever go on that motor launch?" enquired young David. He made a light-hearted comment about leaving the water to the navy.

"Do you want another cup of tea?" said Hannah lifting the pot to see how much was left in it. He didn't and thanked her for a lovely breakfast. David winked at him. He knew their secret was safe.

"Well, if you are done here," said Mr Treluckey, "I'll drop you back in to Padstow now as I've got to take Elizabeth down to get her train, before I get on with my jobs on the farm."

The Major gathered his tie and jacket, folded up the blanket he'd been loaned, said his "Thank you's", and followed Mr Treluckey and his daughter out to the car. Hannah and David came to say goodbye to Elizabeth looking splendid in her new ATS uniform. The Major, sat in the back seat – he'd insisted Elizabeth took the front seat – turned and gave a wave through the rear window of the car.

Mr Treluckey dropped him at the entrance of the Metropole. He thanked him for his assistance and the family's kindness and said he hoped to see them again sometime. He stood and watched as the car descended the short hill to the station entrance. He saw father and daughter embrace before Mr Treluckey got back in the car to return to the farm. The Major lingered no longer and had disappeared into the hotel by the time the farmer's car passed the entrance. He went to the desk and asked for two phone calls

Chapter 8

The call to London simply revealed that his superiors had identified a potential replacement Intelligence Officer for Carlyle. It was a lieutenant in the Royal Engineers, a family man who lived in Plymouth, but who was currently working on the Axminster to Bridgewater Stop Line. They were sending a man to go and meet him. They were relieved to hear from the Major. Apparently an army camp on the north Cornish coast had been bombed yesterday with over 20 killed and many more injured. It seemed it was being used by a Regiment that had suffered badly at Dunkirk. The Major said he'd heard and seen nothing.

"Quick work on the replacement," thought the Major as he replaced the receiver and waited for his second call to be put through.

Captain Cregoe was very excited when the Major eventually got him on the other end of the line.

"He's here. In Bodmin. The killer."

"How do you know?" asked the Major surprised at this unexpected turn of events.

"He's been back to the house and shot one of my men. Seems he came back for some kind of case. He was last seen going into the station opposite. I've got a search party going through the station and goods yard now. I was just about to go and supervise when I was summoned back to the phone."

"I'll be back as soon as I can," said the Major slamming the phone back down and turning and running for the exit. As he emerged from the Metropole he could see the train was still standing at the platform. He ran down the road. He heard a shrill whistle. The guard was signalling for the train to leave. He dashed across the road, through the booking hall, and out onto the platform. The train had begun to pull away, the engine sending great puffs of smoke and soot into the air as it did so. He kept running.

The porter shouted at him "You've missed that one sir! Next one is in an hour." But the Major didn't hear him. His vision was fixed on the final carriage. His heart was pounding. His legs were carrying him as fast as they could. Just as the platform began to slope away he had drawn level with the back of the train and he leapt for it. He slammed into the side of the coach and managed to get one foot on the step and grabbed for the handle with his right hand whilst his left arm stretched round the back of the coach and groped for anything to grab hold of. He teetered there for a moment, watched by the incredulous porter, when suddenly the window was lowered and a pair of hands grabbed at his shoulders and pulled him inwards. He was able to adjust his footing, making it more secure, and then open the door and squeeze inside.

"If you had said you wanted to catch this train, I'd have made the guard keep it for you," said a voice that he thought sounded familiar. The Major, chest heaving, as he sought to recapture his breath, could only smile. Elizabeth led the way back to her compartment.

"Lucky for you I was in the last compartment. It's my secret arrangement with David so he can wave to me from one of our fields that comes down to the railway. This way he'll always know where to look for me on the train," explained Elizabeth.

The Major sat opposite her. "I am so glad you did. I wasn't sure how much longer I would have been able to hold on."

"When I saw you running along the platform I at first wondered what you were doing. But when you kept going I thought I'd better go to the door. That porter's face was a picture when you leaped onto the train." Elizabeth's eyes were smiling.

"So what brought about a sudden change of plan? Not me, I hope." Her expression told the Major she was teasing.

"On this occasion, no," said the Major. "Not that you wouldn't be a worthy cause for such dramatics. No, a phone call brings me back to Bodmin and I didn't want to wait for the next train."

"Well, I shall be delighted to have your company," said Elizabeth genuinely. She had taken to this army officer who had descended so unexpectedly into the church service last evening. Even her mother had remarked before they'd gone to bed that the evening was the first time she'd seen her smile since the sad news last October, and a mother's intuition had told her it was due to the handsome soldier. Elizabeth had blushed but merely replied wondering where on earth this Major had gone with their father at so late an hour. The mystery had grown when she found the Major was back there for breakfast but neither man had said anything of the previous night and she knew it was not her place to ask. The Major had been the perfect gentlemen allowing her to ride alongside her father on the short drive back into Padstow and with the briefest of goodbyes he was gone, although she did glance back and notice he was watching the car descend the hill to the station. But now, she had him to herself. No family in the way. It would be forty minutes before the train pulled into Bodmin. And how she hoped no one would join them in their compartment.

She looked at the Major. He was taking his cap off and running his hand through his blond hair. She was amazed the cap had stayed on during his daring leap. His fingers were long and thick. His hands, she glanced down at hers, were huge by comparison. She rubbed the finger where until this morning her engagement ring had sat. She had put it on a necklace and draped it over the photo of the sailor on the sideboard. 'A time to mourn and a time to dance' she had told herself as she resolved life must go on. The arrival of the Major had helped with that resolution and she looked up at this new interesting character that had descended on her family last evening. He was clean shaven, although some slight stubble revealed he had not shaved this morning. It reminded her of her embarrassment when she had called him for breakfast. But she had been impressed with his athletic frame, and his uniform, while masking something of the muscular build, sat comfortably upon it.

Her silent appreciation was interrupted by his question: "Does this train go to Bodmin Southern or to Bodmin General?"

"Bodmin General. That's why I take this one. It saves the walk across town back to the Depot."

"That's good," he said.

"It's only about one in three that do that. The other Bodmin trains run through to Bodmin Southern," said Elizabeth exhausting her knowledge of the intricacies of the railway timetable.

She moved along the seat to the window, and as the train rounded the curve and emerged from the cutting to cross the iron bridge she began to wave. There was her young brother about fifty yards away in a field up on the hill waving for all he was worth, one of the farm dogs jumping and barking at his side. The Major leaned forward and waved as well. When David spotted someone else waving as well he waved with both hands. The train pulled round the curve and Elizabeth sank back into her seat.

"He's a great younger brother," the Major ventured. Elizabeth, feeling the knot of homesickness in her stomach common to many a service man or woman returning to duty after leave at home, sighed and said, "Yes, he is. He can be mischievous at times but he's loyal, and he's beginning to become more and more useful to my parents on the farm."

"Well I don't mind saying I have thoroughly enjoyed my brief encounter with your family this weekend." Elizabeth beamed. The Major was pleased that his words were well received. He knew that few and far between were the homes you could walk into and feel instantly accepted and at home. He had warmed to this family, and while he knew that an attraction to the daughter might be part of it, he knew it was more than just that. He had the utmost respect for anyone who was joining the Auxiliary Units and sensed they had recruited a capable man in Francis Treluckey. Both he and his wife, Hannah, struck the Major as being people of purpose. They knew what they were about and that gave them an air of confidence the Major admired. Even little David seemed a happy and secure lad and his boyish sense of humour reminded the Major of himself at that age. The final member of the family, Elizabeth, was a young woman of poise, determination, and courage, especially given her loss. The Major looked across the compartment at his beautiful companion. She looked stunning in her uniform. He longed to tell her how he felt, but he was too much of a gentleman to take advantage of one who was getting over the tragic death of a fiancé. He was too much of a man to notice that her ring finger no longer carried the symbol of her pledge to the sailor who had gone over the bar. 'The first move will have to be hers,' he thought, 'but at least she's happy to have me here.'

"It's been lovely to meet you too," Elizabeth said, "even if you do keep my father out to goodness knows what hour." She paused to see if there was any reaction to her comment, but apart from one blink the Major's expression didn't change.

"Oh I heard you come back and clean up at the tap in the yard by the milking shed," she continued. When she saw her words were not provoking any reaction let alone an explanation she decided it was time to change the subject. She knew she'd overstepped the mark. "I bought a Western Morning News at the station if you'd like a glance."

"Yes please," said the Major taking the proffered newspaper wondering whether he would find any report of the events at the army camp. He scanned quickly through the pages and settled on an article talking of the death toll in the air raids. It seemed there had been two raids. The first had been on Saturday which from the description given the Major guessed was Plymouth even though the censor had only allowed the reporting of a raid on a south-west town. The paper spoke of three fatalities there with a handful more casualties being detained at the local hospital. The second seems to have been on Sunday in what the paper described as a south-west coast town. The Major scoured the article for clues of its location but could only find that a number of civilians had been killed and not all the bodies had been recovered. It spoke of local anti-aircraft guns being in action. The Major knew if this was in Cornwall then it had to be Falmouth. Apart from a few on the Cornish side of the Tamar helping to defend the Naval Dockyard at Devonport, Falmouth was the only other town that had any that were operational. Otherwise it would be the aerodrome at St Eval but that wouldn't be described as a coastal town.

"Your brother said he saw some Spitfires yesterday didn't he?" the Major enquired looking up from the paper.

"Yes I think he said something about seeing some rise from St Eval. Must have been about tea time I think."

"Seems they went and chased off the bombers that had raided Falmouth," said the Major.

"Anyone killed?"

"Looks like five from what it says here. All from the same family."

"How awful!" Elizabeth mulled over the fact that the war had now arrived in her own county. This was no longer a war about faraway places that you read about in the papers or heard on the nine o'clock news on the wireless. This was no longer a war that took those you loved from you on the seas. This was war on your doorstep. She shivered and asked the Major, "Do you think the Germans will really invade?

"That seems to be their intention," said the Major without looking up from the paper.

"But here in Cornwall? Why are they attacking Cornwall? Will they invade here?"

The Major sensed the vulnerability in her voice and folded the paper and put it on the seat. "They could attack anywhere from Cornwall to Newcastle. That's why we need to be ready and vigilant. Every town, every village, every beach needs to be guarded. That's why your father has joined the LDV, isn't it? And if Jerry lands here in Cornwall I'm sure he won't be made very welcome!"

"Too right!" Elizabeth exclaimed her eyes wide. "I don't like the idea of killing but this evil dictator needs to be stopped at all costs. I'm sure if the army let me have a gun I'd shoot a few, especially after what they did to my ..." She stopped as if she dare not say his name. Her eyes moistened. "Well it's not going to bring him back. What is this world coming to, Major?"

"I don't know," said the Major truthfully. "J.S. Mill once said at St Andrews 'Bad men need nothing more to compass their ends than that good men should look on and do nothing.' At least the good men of Britain are now doing something, even if we should have done it years ago when stopping Hitler would have been easier."

"He certainly needs to be stopped. I have read of what he's done to so many of his own people in Germany. And to the Jews, hounding them out of their jobs and businesses. No wonder so many left."

Now it was the Major's turn to go quiet. He thought of the family on the photograph in his pocket and the letter from Vienna. If only they'd left. The pangs of guilt swept over the Major.

"I hate the Nazis," he said with such feeling that Elizabeth wondered just what was behind those words. She sensed it was to do with his brother and family and remembering the haunted look on the Major's face when she'd asked about family the previous evening she knew she should tread lightly.

"We will win. Now Churchill's in charge. As he's said 'We will never surrender!' We are all doing our bit and we will pull through."

The Major smiled. "You are just what I need," he said. He could have reached across and kissed her, but instead he just gave her back the newspaper.

The train gave a jolt. It was pulling away from the tiny halt at Nanstallon. The Major had missed so much of the journey. He could vaguely remember stopping at Wadebridge as the Station Manager had shouted the name as the signs declaring the place name had been removed, but he wondered how many of the other halts through the valley up from Wadebridge they had stopped at. The engine was now straining as they began the long climb from Boscarne Junction up to Bodmin General. A few minutes more and his time with Elizabeth would be over. He took some paper and a pencil from his jacket pocket and scribbled something down.

"I am going to have to run and leave you as soon as we arrive," he said, his mind beginning to refocus on the task that had brought him racing back to Bodmin. "But here are my details and I can be contacted on this number at the Depot. I would be honoured if I could take you to dinner some time, if you'd agree to see me again."

Elizabeth read what was on the paper and looked up. "I would be delighted," she said, her eyes smiling.

"That's spiffing!" The Major was smiling too.

"But do take care. I don't want you getting off the train in as much hurry as you got on it." She was teasing him again.

"I will do my best."

She carefully folded the piece of paper and put it in her pocket. The Major stood.

"I really do have to run, so I will say goodbye now." Elizabeth stood as well and he reached out a hand to shake hers but she clasped his elbow and pulled him close and planted a kiss on his cheek. She then glanced at his face, still holding his arm, to see his reaction. She feared she had been too forward. She had never acted in such a way before, not even with her fiancé. He said nothing but put his arm round her, pulled her into him and kissed her on the lips. She felt a tingle all over and let herself be consumed by his unexpected but most welcome display of affection. The train was now on the curve into Bodmin General and the barracks came into view before disappearing from sight as they passed under the final road bridge.

"Got to dash," he said grabbing his cap and disappeared out into the corridor. The train slowed as it pulled alongside the signal box and into the platform. She noticed there were soldiers on the platform, and as she glanced in the other direction, in the goods yard as well. Then she saw the Major fly past the window. He had jumped off the train before it had stopped. She laughed to herself and shook her head. She made her way out to the exit, and as she alighted on to the platform she saw the Major talking to another officer before she was directed along the platform by one of the soldiers.

"What's going on?" she asked.

"Just searching for someone, miss," said the trooper, his rifle in his hands. "Now if you could leave the station through the booking hall immediately, it would be most helpful. Thank you, miss."

With one last look back at the Major Elizabeth exited the station and headed back to the Depot.

Chapter 9

Captain Cregoe was on the platform waiting for Major Trevennel when the Padstow train pulled in.

"I guessed you were on your way when you hung up on me on the telephone," the Captain laughed.

"So what's the news? Where's this chap gone?" the Major asked.

"We have searched the station and the goods yard and not found him. My men have gone through the rhododendrons on the bank up to Harleigh Road, and scoured the undergrowth up as far as the bridges, but there's no sight of him."

"How many trains have left the station?"

"Yours is the first one in the station since our phone call."

"If he's not here then which way did he get out?" The Major was thinking aloud. "Down by the engine shed beyond the signal box there are steps that go up to the road and come out by the school. Could he have used those?"

"No, we asked the men working in the shed and they said no one had been past. They were working on the coupling at the front of the engine there so anyone going up the steps would have had to walk right past them."

"Excuse me," the Major was calling to a porter on the platform who was wheeling a trolley load of luggage to the train.

"Yes sir," the porter said gently standing his trolley upright so the cases on it wouldn't fall off.

"Have there been any goods trains this morning? I mean have any left from here?"

"The coal train went back down to Bodmin Road 'bout fifty minutes ago. It's only four wagons and a brake van."

The Major and the Captain looked at each other. "That's it!" they said in unison.

"What's the best way to get there?" said the Captain. "Shall I go to the depot and get transport?"

"No this one is about to leave. It goes down to Bodmin Road before going back to Padstow." They boarded the train.

"You take the window on that side and I'll look out this one just to make sure there's no sign of him between here and there," said the Major.

"You don't think he'll have caught a train on the main line and be well gone by the time we get there."

"This is Cornwall, Captain. Trains aren't that frequent. Besides they are usually timed to meet the branch line connections, and that's the one we are on. Hopefully we will be in luck."

The porter had finished loading his cases. The guard blew his whistle and with a hiss of steam from the engine the train began to move. The engine had run around while they had been talking on the platform and now it headed under the left hand arch at the end of the station. The Captain had a grand view of the barracks as the hill sloped away and the train was riding high on the embankment. The Major looked out onto green fields. He could see the line he'd just travelled as it snaked round the Beacon and out of sight. As the train crossed the bridge over the Lostwithiel road he could see the Grammar School sports field and then he was looking at the backs of a line of houses built by the town corporation.

Although both men kept their eyes peeled there was no sign of their prey. Quite what they expected to see if he had jumped from the goods train is uncertain, but they enjoyed the scenic descent into the Glynn Valley. Past cottages and farms, woods and fields, hedges and fences and then a sixty foot drop from the viaduct down to the River Fowey just as the train whistled and slowed to enter Bodmin Road station.

The small tank engine hissed as it came to a halt. The station was in the wooded Glynn valley next to the River Fowey that ran from moor to sea. The line had been built by Brunel four and half miles from the town it served as the landowners and towns people conspired against the new innovation to protect their interest in the coach and horses traffic. It seems the company could not raise the money locally. It was not until the 1880's that the town had been linked to the mainline when a new generation of businessmen realised what a mistake their predecessors had made. It was somewhat ironic when one considers that the Bodmin – Wadebridge Railway opened in 1834 was the first passenger line south of Liverpool at that time! But to connect Bodmin to the outside world in 1859 – that was a step too far for the short-sighted, self-interested investors.

The Major and Captain were among a dozen or so passengers that alighted. The Major stepped away from the train so he could scan everyone else getting off: an elderly gentleman with a stick, a mother and child aged about eight, a man in a trilby hat who looked like a travelling salesman, a couple of lads in shorts with notebooks in hand obviously here for a bit of trainspotting, a sailor with a kitbag heading to or from leave, one or two others but no sign of their man.

The Captain meanwhile was taking in the handful of passengers waiting on the down platform. There were two women in summer dresses, perhaps aged in their fifties, handbags over their arms, a man in overalls who from the dusting on them had just completed a shift at the china clay dry just beyond the railway cottages to the west of the station, and a young man with blonde hair who had turned and seemed to be examining the signal box.

The sound of an approaching train could be heard coming from the east as it rounded the curve below Newbridge Wood. "That's him," said the Captain in low tones so only the Major would hear. The Major turned and for the first time saw his prey. He was blonde, about six feet tall, an athletic frame not dissimilar to the Major. He looked well-dressed except for a black stain on his back. Coal dust. As if sensing he was being watched, he turned and looked across to their platform.

"We need to get him before that train arrives," said the Captain. The young man was watching them now. He knew he was the subject of their discussion although across the double track he could not hear what was being said. The Major and the Captain turned and ran for the footbridge. Its wooden steps creaked as they bounded up them two at a time. The train was entering the station now. As they crossed the footbridge the Major glanced out of the windows down on to the platform. The young man was stood quickly looking this way and that and running his hand through his hair. He disappeared from sight as they turned left to descend the steps to the down platform. The engine was showing no signs of stopping and as they emerged from the bridge they could see it was a goods train. They swung round towards their prey. He saw them coming. He hesitated for a moment and then turned and ran along the platform. The Major and the Captain gave chase. The women stopped their conversation and looked up. "Stop him!" shouted the Captain. The clay worker heard and moved to block the exit from the platform. However the young man running towards him drew a pistol and fired as he ran at him. The bullet was high. It smashed a window in the waiting room but it was enough to convince the clay worker discretion was the better part of valour and he threw himself back against the waiting room wall. The women screamed as the Captain passed them with the Major a pace or two behind. But it was not the young man's intention to exit the station, or even to head into the goods yard. With a flying leap he hurled himself at one of the wooden plank wagons as it passed him and with a thud landed half on, half off. With a kick of his legs he wriggled on to the tarpaulin covering the truck. The Captain stopped. The quarry was gone. But the Major was not giving up that easily. A couple of horse box and other assorted wagons came by before there was another series of plank wagons. The Major kept running and then leapt at one of them. His cap flew off and landed on the platform. He grabbed at anything he could and managed to hold on. He swung his legs over onto the tarpaulin, and rolled over onto his back gasping for air. "I have got to stop catching trains in this fashion," he told himself.

The Captain stood in absolute disbelief at the scene he had just witnessed. The train, which had slowed to pass through the station, was now accelerating as it dropped down the incline towards Respryn. The Captain turned and waved and shouted at the Guard's van. The Guard was stood in the veranda of his Toad brake van but because of the curve of the track through Bodmin Road station and the larger wagons in front of him he had not seen a thing. He merely waved at what he thought was a rather exuberant soldier waving on the platform, unable to hear above the clanking of the trucks and the squeal of metal on rails on the curve. The Captain stood hands on hips watching the train disappear out of sight. He slowly walked and picked the Major's cap up aware that all eyes on both sides of the station were on him. He turned back towards the startled passengers on the down platform and asked if everyone was all right. A railway employee had emerged and was wondering what had broken the window. He seemed unaware that it was a gunshot. When they started to ask questions altogether of the Captain he merely said, "Excuse me," and made his way to the signal box. On the up platform the passengers had begun to talk but the two schoolboys stood transfixed. Trainspotting was usually not this exciting not even when you were collecting 'namers'. The Captain climbed the steps and opened the door.

"Where's that train going?" he asked the somewhat startled signalman.

"I don't know," came the reply.

"You must know, you're the signalman!" said an incredulous Captain. The signalman turned and faced his questioner. He looked the uniform up and down before replying again.

"Well it's going down the line, and I've passed it over to the Lostwithiel box, and as there be no junctions between here and there I'd say it's at least going to Lostwithiel, but where 'tis headed after that, it's not for the likes of me to know. It's a military train, see, and there's been so many of them this past six weeks I can no keep track of 'em."

"Who will know?" demanded the Captain.

"The army or the navy or the air force, I expect. Depends which one of them had that train."

"So which was it? Don't you get told what's coming?"

"Three bells from the Onslow box. That's all I'm told. That tells me a train is coming, I have no idea who it belongs to, unless it is one of the regular scheduled services. I'm only a humble signalman. I keeps 'em safe, see, I'm not the one who…"

"I need to use your phone," interrupted the Captain looking around to find it.

"That's only for emergencies," said the signalman.

"This *is* an emergency," said the increasingly exasperated Captain. "Didn't you see what happened, man?" The railwayman looked blankly surprised.

"I acknowledged the driver's wave, and then I pulled the levers for the signals and rang the bells for the Lostwithiel box," he said somewhat bemused.

"An enemy suspect jumped onto one of the wagons, and so the Major did the same to continue the chase." The railwayman's eyes were wide open in utter amazement. He had missed the drama completely. He pointed to the phone.

"How do I get connected to the operator rather than the railway system?" the Captain asked, sinking down onto a seat next to the desk. "I need to speak to the Depot at Bodmin."

Chapter 10

The Major lay where he was for a moment sizing up his options. Further ahead on this train was an armed enemy. He was dangerous: the Captain had already explained how he had shot at one of his men at the house in St Nicholas Street. He was probably responsible for the deaths of two men: Corporal Miller at the same house in Bodmin and Lieutenant Carlyle at the Auxiliary Unit hideout near Padstow. Now he had fired at an unarmed civilian in broad daylight. The Major checked his revolver. It was his trusty Enfield 2. It was fully loaded. He would have six shots and knew he would stop anyone at a range of up to 14 yards. His hand went to a pocket in his tunic. He had some spare cartridges.

"I could go and get the guard to stop the train, but that would only give him chance to make a run for it," the Major said to himself. "Jumping off a moving train is certainly more risky than jumping on, so unless he wants a broken leg or ankle or perhaps worse, then he's likely to stay on for the time being." The Major rose to his knees.

"The best plan of action is to locate him on the train and neutralise him. Perhaps a good shot would disarm him. It would be better to take him alive. Then we can question him about his activities. Hopefully Cregoe will be summoning help. Right, best foot forward."

The Major stood up. The wind rushed through his hair. He looked around at the fields either side. A little further to his right there was a river. The treeline grew closer. Suddenly his whole horizon darkened and he instinctively dived down as the train entered the portal of a tunnel. Now he knew where he was. This had to be Brownqueen Tunnel. It wasn't long, just 88 yards, but it was notorious. The Major recalled reading the story of Silvanus Trevail, the Cornish architect who had built many schools around the county as well as the Headland Hotel in Newquay and the Asylum in Bodmin. Suffering from depression, this President of the Royal Society of Architects had taken the 11:40 up train on 7 November 1903, left his seat at Par Station, and then as the train was going through the tunnel, shot himself in the lavatory. Passengers had called a porter when the train stopped at Bodmin Road and Trevail's body was found lying across the toilet. No shots were heard on this journey. The train exited the tunnel and the Major again stood up. With a wobble or two he made his way forward to the edge of the wagon. He placed his right foot on top of the front plank to give him leverage, and leapt forward, revolver in hand, onto the next wagon. He swayed a couple of times, but his confidence was growing and he managed the five plank wagons without mishap.

Next was a covered carriage truck. In Great Western Railway parlance this was known as a Mink G. It was thirty feet long and capable of carrying 20 tons. Gingerly the Major climbed over the end of the last plank wagon and rested a foot on the buffer. He looked down to be sure of his footing and was alarmed at the speed with which the sleepers were passing underneath. Concentrating on the task in hand, rather than his fears, the Major stepped across to the CCT buffer and was able to stand on the narrow ridge. A quick glance around one side of the wagon made him decide the safest way to traverse this obstacle was across its roof. He did notice that someone had chalked a "Z" on the loading board, but he was unaware that this was GWR code for a gunpowder wagon. His hands reached along the iron frame and using the diagonal slat was able to get some purchase to push himself up. His hands grasped the roof and, with a test of strength for his arms, he was able to pull himself up on to the top of the wagon. He knelt up, and then just as quickly dived flat as the train passed under a bridge. He looked about him to get his bearings. To the right was Restormel Manor, a seventeenth century farmhouse, and there on the hill above the medieval ruin of Restormel Castle, standing as a majestic sentinel over the valley.

"Good," thought the Major, "no more bridges for a while." He stood up and began to walk along the roof. He could see the River Fowey down to his right. The small town of Lostwithiel where he had been just a couple of days earlier was coming into view. He jumped onto the next wagon and looked ahead. There was neither sight nor sign of his target. Then he remembered the new road and bridge at Lostwithiel. That was where he had first met Captain Cregoe. It had only been built in 1939 which is why he hadn't thought of it immediately. He decided to lie down. He didn't know how trigger happy Cregoe's men guarding Lostwithiel would be and decided it was best not to attract attention to himself unless it was obvious Cregoe had phoned ahead and help was on hand. Surely the train slowing and stopping at a signal would be the first sign of that. Lostwithiel station with the Worcesters building the defences in the town would be the obvious opportunity to stop the train at a place where assistance was available.

The train passed under the new road bridge. The Major could see some soldiers by the new pillbox but they took no notice of the train. It passed the Lostwithiel Dairy and then was hurtling across the level crossing. The gates were keeping back a car and a handful of pedestrians but none seemed to notice the figure spread-eagled on top of one of the covered carriage trucks.

"There is no help here," thought the Major as the train passed through the station without stopping. The train for Fowey stood waiting in its platform on the south side of the station. "Perhaps it's too soon. Cregoe couldn't have got assistance that quick." The Major knew he was on his own and his mind reverted to his original plan.

He edged his way forward on the top of the truck. He raised himself up and jumped to the front of the CCT's. He decided to crawl along this last one just in case his enemy had spotted him. The engine was now working hard as it climbed the hill up from Lostwithiel. He was glad he was crawling as it passed under another bridge just before crossing the Milltown viaduct. He looked down on the tidy cottage garden way below him. He was getting covered in smuts from the smoke now pouring from the engine.

He reached the end of the thirty foot truck and looked ahead along the line of trucks. There were a number of plank wagons, a couple of flatbeds with what looked like field guns under tarpaulins, before some more plank wagons and then a final covered carriage truck before the engine and tender. The Major couldn't see that the engine was 5020 Trematon Castle, built in 1932, but he knew it was certainly man enough to haul this goods train up the steep Cornish banks at speed. He looked for any sign of his quarry. In the first series of plank wagons he could see a tarpaulin that was heavily indented. That had to be where his prey had landed on taking that flying leap at Bodmin Road. There was no sign of him now. His gaze moved forwards. Nothing seemed out of place. He focused on the two flatbed trucks each with two guns under tarpaulins. They did not look as if they would provide sufficient hiding places. All of a sudden he was pitched into darkness as the train reached the summit and entered Treverrin Tunnel. The smoke swirled around him and he coughed. He shut his eyes to protect them from the smuts. On and on this tunnel seemed to go. He coughed again. He was struggling for breath when at last the 565 yards were up and they broke once more into daylight and the air around him cleared. His throat burned, and he exhaled deeply before opening his mouth and gasped for breath. He opened his eyes with a shake of his head. They were heading down the valley towards Par. His eyes continued forward. More plank trucks. He surveyed them one by one. There on the fourth truck along, flapping in the breeze, was a loose rope. The tarpaulin was loose on one corner. That had to be the truck he was in. He had located his target.

He was out of range perched here on the roof of the truck. He swung round and dipped his legs over the side feeling for the iron bars that would give him a foothold. He gingerly worked his way down on to the buffers and climbed on to the first of the plank wagons. The tarpaulin sank slightly under his weight and he lay there as they went under the road bridge at Par station. The train showed no sign of slowing. This train had obviously been signalled through. "Trust the efficiency of the Great Western Railway," he mused to himself. There was no sign of any military presence on the platform as they rushed through the station at about forty five miles an hour. The train was now climbing again and he could see the Fowey branch line pass underneath them and the clear blue water of Par Docks to his left until it disappeared behind the trees.

He got up once more and continued clambering over the plank wagons taking his time. He doubted whether his target would hear him approaching above the noise of the engine and the rush of the air as they continued at speed under another farm bridge and then along the embankment with a glorious view right across St Austell Bay past the prestigious Carlyon Bay hotel. He had reached the last one as they crossed the St Austell road on a bridge and he could see the scattered hamlets and china clay works on the hill above the town. He decided he would be better off staying here as they passed through St Austell station, especially if Cregoe had been able to summon assistance, even if it was only the Cornish Constabulary. 'A Cornish bobby would be better than no one,' he thought. 'Mind you, this villain has already shown he will shoot at anyone even if they are not armed.'

They rumbled on and straight through the station. There was a sprinkling of people on the platforms but few took much notice of the goods train as it hurtled through. The Major began to wonder just where they might end up. He was certain from the guns on the flatbeds this had to be a supply train for the army, but where in Cornwall would be its destination. Penzance, Falmouth, Truro, to be honest, it could be anywhere. Reinforcements had been pouring into Cornwall since Dunkirk. Some were units regrouping and being made up to strength again. Some like the Captain's men had been sent to build the defences that would see off the invasion when it came. This train could be going to any one of them.

As the train crossed a couple of viaducts with houses and china clay works in the valleys below, the Major again began to move. He climbed over the end of the plank wagon and jumped from the buffers on to the flatbed truck. Holding onto the tarpaulins covering the guns he was able to traverse them quickly without too much difficulty. He had just jumped onto the second flatbed when he sensed the train begin to slow. He looked down. They were crossing over a main road on a bridge. Houses lined the road in both directions. They rounded a curve slowing all the time. The Major could see some sidings off to the right by the china clay dries. He recognised them from his journeys on the line but he couldn't put a name to them.

He squatted down between the two guns on this front flatbed. He was unsure whether the slowing would bring his quarry out from his hiding place. He knew he needed to be ready in case his enemy took advantage of the slower speed to jump from the train. The Major estimated they had slowed to about twenty miles per hour as they passed the old station house, and then he heard the clanking and squealing of the wheels as they traversed the points, firstly onto the up track, and then again on to the branch line. The Major knew this line from the Junction headed up through clay country towards St Dennis.

Again the signals permitted them to pass straight through. "Military trains must be receiving priority," he thought. "Another sign the country is waking up to the realities of imminent invasion." The wagons creaked and groaned as they wound their way up the curves of the branch line. He estimated the train was now doing a steady twenty five miles per hour, maybe thirty maximum.

He peered round the side of the gun holding onto one of the ropes keeping the tarpaulin place. There staring back at him from four trucks along was his quarry. Both went for their weapons at the same time. There was an exchange of shots.

91

Neither was very accurate, but it caused the Major to dodge back behind the gun. He peered round again and could see the top of a man's head gingerly rising to peer over the end of the plank wagon. He took aim, more carefully this time. His finger tightened on the trigger and just as two eyes appeared he fired. The bullet struck the plank wagon on one of the iron supports and deflected off to the side. The head immediately disappeared from sight. Just as the Major considered advancing even closer his target stood and using two hands to steady his aim fired several shots at him. The Major thrust himself back behind the gun as it was his turn to hear bullets ricocheting off metal. When the pistol fell silent the Major edged round to have another look. No sign of the man. The Major could see some movement on the tarpaulin and wondered whether he could be reloading. Seizing his chance, he leapt forward round the gun and towards the plank wagon. Just as he was negotiating the buffers to step from the flatbed to the plank wagon, the blonde head appeared again, and straight away an arm came up. The Major saw the flash from the muzzle and thought he would be hit. However at just that moment the train lurched on the curve and he fell backwards onto the flatbed. The bullet hit the gun behind him and flew off at an angle. Sensing he had hit the Major the adversary stood to try and see him and fired again as the Major scrambled back along the flatbed for the protection of the wrapped up gun. A bullet whizzed past his ear but he was not hit. The Major was panting as he got back to his haunches. Now was his chance to return fire as his prey was still standing in the wagon. He fired two shots but the young man dived for cover in the protection of his truck. The Major paused to catch his breath.

Chapter 11

Johann breathed heavily as he reloaded. His fingers fumbled and he told himself to 'Calm down'. Clear, incisive, almost instinctive, thinking had guided him through his training and that is what he needed now. The mission had gone well. The quality of the information he had gathered would surely impress them at 76 Tirpitzufer. All until that silly girl had almost spoiled everything. Why had he allowed himself to become so embroiled? 'Use the locals as cover' his training had said, 'but don't become so engaged in their lives or emotionally attached that you compromise your very important work.' His mind flashed back to the first time he had seen her. She was descending the stairs at his lodgings wearing a rather short skirt and from his viewpoint at the foot of the stairs she seemed to flaunt her long legs with every slow step. As she passed him he found himself remarking "You've got beautiful legs!" She was beautiful. The rest of that day he had been unable to get her well-endowed figure out of his mind.

He had lain in his bed that night thinking she was not like the girls back home. With their braided hair and pinafores they appeared so plain, so dull, so monochrome. She was sassy, playful. He was sure she was flirting with him on the stairs, but he was only here for a couple of weeks. The mission came first and he needed to put her out of his mind. He turned over and pulled the blanket up.

He had then heard a creaking but it had taken a moment before he realised that the noise was his door opening. His head shot round wondering where he had left his pistol when he saw it was Kara stood there in a silk dressing gown. He sat up in the bed. She lifted a foot on to the bottom of the bed so the dressing gown parted revealing a leg. He had glanced at her thigh and then up at her face.

'So you like my legs?' she had whispered. He nodded without saying anything. He looked towards the door wondering if anyone else in the house was aware that she was in his room. If Mrs Johns knew she might sling him out on his hook. That would set the mission back a day or two if he had to relocate.

'Then you will definitely like these," she had smiled as she pulled the tassel on her gown and parted it revealing her ample bosom rising and falling with her breathing. He gasped. He was spellbound. She began to move towards him when there was the sound of a door opening and footsteps on the stairs, and with a swirl she was gone gliding out of his room and back up to the attic where she slept. He lay back on his pillow, his head spinning.

The wheels of the truck squealed as they crossed the points of a siding to a china clay dry. He was reloaded and ready to take out his pursuer. While he told himself no young man in his position would have been able to resist the wiles of Kara's advances, he knew he had been foolish to get her involved in the mission. But a couple of young lovers travelling the county were ignored much more than a foreign young gentleman travelling by himself. English reserve had tutted and muttered about the amorous couple but had not inflicted on him the same scrutiny he had sensed when he had ridden alone. But she had naturally been curious about his work and the places he was taking her. He had invited her to Padstow as she was the perfect cover for him to walk round the port and reconnoitre the estuary's defences. A railway compartment to themselves would have meant a romantic ride until that Mr Carlyle from the lodgings had shown up and asked if he could share the journey. The small talk had soon run out and that's when the problems started. Why had she had to ask so many questions in the railway carriage? The officer was clearly suspicious of them both. He had tried so hard to brush off her questions, to change the topic, but she had persisted. That's why he had had to send her back on the next train much to her annoyance and protests. But he would now have to track Carlyle to see if the mission was compromised.

He had spent the rest of that evening sat in the corner of the railway hotel restaurant as Carlyle had dined with a British Army Major. He had strained to hear their conversation but they spoke in subtle tones that did not carry across to his corner. They had taken a leisurely meal before adjourning to the bar for a drink. The Major seemed pleased with whatever Carlyle was telling him. There didn't appear to be any alarm, so perhaps they had got away with Kara's indiscretions on the train. But he knew Carlyle was certainly suspicious of him. He'd been asking questions in the lodgings, stirring up that Miller fellow to the extent that when Johann found the soldier rifling through his room he had to bring that to a halt. Then was Carlyle's coming to sit in their railway compartment co-incidence or design? If opportunity presented itself he would take it. He couldn't act in the hotel – too many witnesses – but when Carlyle had gone for a walk into the countryside early the next morning he decided this would be the chance to strike. Carlyle was certainly a fast walker and in the hills and bends of the narrow lanes Johann had lost him after a couple of miles. Johann had tried several of the lanes leading from a crossroads but there was no sight of his man, so when he had found himself in a village he headed for the local inn to quench his thirst only to find it didn't open until midday.

He had sat on the bench outside wondering just what to do when he couldn't believe his luck. It had been well over an hour since he last had sight of the officer when only twenty yards from where he was sat Carlyle was shaking hands with a man who appeared to be a local farmer and waving goodbye. Carlyle took the road towards Padstow and Johann was about to get up to follow him, when glancing back several times to see that the farmer had disappeared Carlyle turned around and headed down the lane out of which the duo had emerged. This time Johann had followed a little more closely. When after about a mile Carlyle climbed a gate and headed into a field Johann knew this was his moment. It had been a fortuitous location as the field led into a disused quarry where Carlyle had stopped to examine the entrance to some old quarry workings allowing Johann to pounce without his foe seeing him. He was able to dispose of the body in the underground workings grateful that it would be some considerable time before anyone would find the body in such a remote place. He was able to wash his hands in the nearby stream before setting off back to Padstow. He spent the next day gathering the information he needed on the siting of the defences being constructed around the estuary and had headed out of town on the first train on Monday morning.

It was on his return to Bodmin later that morning when he realised the net was closing around him. There were soldiers stationed at the house. He needed his case, or more importantly the rolls of film within it, and had tried to sneak through the neighbouring gardens to get to the back door. He had managed to retrieve his case and was leaving by the same route he arrived when an upstairs window had been thrown open and he'd been challenged. One shot had sent the soldier falling back into the room clutching his stomach and Johann had vaulted a couple of fences and emerged from the side of a house further up the street having left his case in the unsuspecting householder's dustbin, the rolls of film secured about his person. He had crossed the road and headed into the railway station.

The thought brought him back to his present situation. With his pistol loaded he was ready for action. It was time to see off this Major once and for all. Time to put all thought of the pretty young woman at the lodgings out of his mind. Kara had served her purpose and now it was time to concentrate on getting his information back to his superiors. He climbed to his knees and slowly peered over the top of the wagon.

Chapter 12

A cat and mouse game ensued with each man firing when they thought they had a reasonable chance of hitting the target, but neither risking any move to get closer to ensure success. The train had reached the summit amidst the china clay workings and was now on its descent down to St Dennis Junction. As they came onto the final straight to the junction the Major decided he needed to attract the attention of the signalman. Cregoe had obviously not been able to summon help thus far and he needed to alert someone to the dangers he was facing. Having come this way there was every possibility of the train stopping at St Columb Road or even Newquay if the supplies were for RAF St Eval. St Columb was now just a couple of miles away.

The train was cleared through the junction. A few clay wagons stood in the loop and there was a rake of mineral wagons on a siding on an embankment off to the right. The signalman was leaning out of his open window. The Major shouted. The signalman looked surprised but merely waved back. The Major realised he had not heard a word, so he aimed his revolver at the signal box and fired. The bullet smashed the far window and the signalman dived for cover. The Major watched and saw him emerge in the end window facing them. "Hopefully," thought the Major, "he'll have the sense to phone someone, even if only to complain about being shot at!" The train passed under the A30 bridge and the signal box was lost from sight.

The Major turned his attention back to his quarry. If the train was to stop at St Columb then he needed to be ready to keep his prey stuck in the wagon until help could be summoned. He would have to take the initiative, the Major mused, especially as help may only be in the form of railway employees or the village policeman who, most likely, no, most definitely, would not be armed. The train now passed the point where the original line of the railway went through the Toldish tunnel. It had been bypassed when the line was converted to standard gauge in 1874. The thought struck the Major that such a location would make a very good hideout for an enemy agent seeking to operate in this part of Cornwall. Just what was his quarry up to? Was he spying on the defence preparations? Was he aware of the Auxiliaries? Was he transmitting information back to the Nazis in France? Surely he had more of an operation than a boarding house in Bodmin? Were the Johns Fifth Columnists? It seemed unlikely but he couldn't rule anything out. This young

Dutchman, if that's what he really was, certainly seemed to be using the railways to move about. The Major was full of questions and had few answers.

The train was now on the long curve to bring it back to the line of the original railway the far side of the old tunnel. The Major felt the turn in the opposite direction as they curved round towards the station at St Columb Road. There was no indication the train was slowing down. The Major peered ahead but there was no sign of the blonde haired young man. The train crossed the road bridge and rattled through the deserted station. It began to pick up speed as it rounded the more gentle curves as it made its way ever nearer Newquay. The Major wondered what Cregoe was doing and when any assistance he had organised would emerge. He chuckled to himself as he thought of the frantic call the signalman at St Dennis Junction would have made. Perhaps all would be revealed when they arrived in the north coast terminus. They crossed the level crossing at Quintrell Downs. The gate-keeper stood by the gates watching the train go through as a car and a truck queued on the St Columb Minor side of the crossing. There was nothing in that rural scene to indicate anyone had been informed or suspected that anything was amiss as this long train thundered across. There were a couple more slight curves, another crossing on a lane with the gatekeeper's cottage the only thing in sight.

The Major was steeling himself for a showdown in Newquay when the train slowed and then suddenly lurched to the left. "How could I have forgot? Tolcarn Junction. We are now heading round the Treloggan curve to go down the line towards Perranporth." Perhaps it was the Major's annoyance at not considering all possible destinations, perhaps it was some subconscious cognisance that Perranporth had seen the loss of army life in the bombing on Sunday but he resolved then and there he was going to bring this villain to book. Cometh the hour, cometh the man. England expects every man to do his duty. This was his duty.

The Major peered forwards round the gun. There was still no sign of his quarry. He moved forward once more. He gently climbed over the buffers as the train whistled past a small halt and a level crossing. The gate-keeper looked absolutely amazed to see someone in army uniform on the train. The Major pulled himself onto the first of the plank wagons and clambered over the tarpaulin. He looked down at the next set of buffers he had to negotiate. The ground sped past underneath. The

Major would guess they were now doing a steady thirty miles an hour. He climbed up onto the plank wagon and was crossing the tarpaulin on all fours with his revolver in his right hand. Just as he reached the far end the blonde head popped up from its hiding place. Eyes widened showing the opponent had been startled by this bold approach. An arm came up and the Major fired. He missed. The target fired back but the shot was high. Then the man fired again. Nothing. He reached down to be able to reload. The Major seized his chance. He stood, leapt onto the next wagon and bounced over the tarpaulin and as the young man rose again pistol in hand the Major took a flying leap. His shoulder crashed into the assailant's midriff and flung him back his shot going off wildly into the air. The Major's revolver went sprawling somewhere under the tarpaulin. The two bodies crashed into the boxes stacked under the green cover and the young man groaned. The Major reached for his arm, grabbed it and smashed it down on the rim of the truck. His adversary winced but did not loosen his hold on his weapon. The Major reached across with both hands and repeated the move. Able to bring much force to bear, the Major smashed his hand down on the top of the plank side. The man howled and the pistol fell from his grasp somewhere inside the truck. At this the young man pushed himself up and grabbed the Major and rolled him down onto the tarpaulin. He drew his right hand back and thrust his fist into the Major's chest. The Major felt the blow and moved to block the next one. The Major kicked out at his assailant's legs who then paused to steady himself allowing the Major to propel himself forward smashing his forehead into the man's face, grabbing his arms at the same time and knocking him backwards. The two of them fell into the space beneath the loosened tarpaulin entwined, grabbling with each other, and both trying to get the hold that would give them the edge in this desperate combat. Neither saw nor felt a weapon that would bring it to an end.

The young man got a hand free which he pushed into the Major's face pushing his head back. The foe was strong. He pushed and pushed, and the Major felt his back arching. The man suddenly let go, moved back and used the space to bring his knee up into the Major's groin. Now it was the Major's chance to groan. The young man seized his chance and began to clamber up out of the truck. The major reached forward and grabbed an ankle and jerked it backwards causing his opponent to fall across the ends of the two trucks. The Major stood and tried to tip him into the space between the two. The young man, however, had a strong grip with his hands on the other truck and was able to kick out, knocking the Major backwards once more. The enemy pulled himself up and leapt at the Major raining blows down on his head. The Major grabbed him close like a boxer in the ring and the two wrestled this way and that trying to achieve the advantageous grip. The two were oblivious to the fact that the train was passing the old engine house of East Wheal Rose and then shortly crossed a road bridge and passed the platform for Mitchell & Newlyn. Not that there was anyone at the Halt to witness the grappling pair pass by.

The Major grunted as he took a punch in the stomach. He pushed his hand under the younger man's nose and jerked his head back. This war had suddenly become personal. It was kill or be killed. The Major had never met this fellow before but here was a fight to the death. This was not some remote engagement firing rounds from the turret of a tank or pulling a lever to release bombs thousands of feet above a target. Like two gladiators fighting in the arena, the two men grappled and punched and fought in the confines of the truck. As the Major glared into the whites of his opponent's eyes the thought went through his mind "I have never seen you before or done anything to you or your family, yet you believe in an ideology so warped but so powerful that you will come to my country to kill, to destroy and to seek to take away the freedoms that I and my people hold so precious." The Major's thoughts turned to anger. "Who do you think you are? What gives you the right? Right now you are the face of evil and you will be defeated."

The Major felt a surge of strength and he grabbed this personification of anathema round the neck and tightened his grip. Thoughts of his brother and his young family in Vienna flashed through his mind. Hatred of all this man stood for and was doing surged through the Major's veins. He squeezed. The young man's face had turned white in fear at this new vicious assault. His legs seemed to give way beneath him and he slumped to the floor of the truck, the Major's hands still round his throat. The opponent's hands flailed about. All of a sudden his hands touched something on the floor of the truck. He wrapped his fingers around it. It was the wooden grip of his pistol. The Prague made Ceska Zbrojovka vz.27 or the Pistole Modell 27 as it had been introduced to him by the officer back in training. He eased his fingers round the grip, slid his firing finger onto the trigger, turned the muzzle up towards the Major and squeezed.

The Major felt a hot searing pain in his left arm. He yelled as he let his grip go on the young man's neck. The young man pushed him back and with pistol still in hand vaulted the side of the truck. The train had slowed as it was taking the points at the junction at Shepherd's to turn onto the Treamble branch line. Its speed was no more than ten miles per hour. The victor turned back towards the truck, raised his pistol, hesitated, and then turned and ran across the tracks, up the steps of the cattle pen and started climbing over the fence towards the road.

The Major, realised he was fortunate to have escaped with just a wound to his arm and not to have received a fatal shot, groped around with his good arm and found his pistol. He shakily stood up in the truck and saw the young man legs astride on the wooden fence. He fired but as the train was moving behind the up platform on the branch he had little chance of hitting his target. The shooting did bring two railway employees rushing out of the station building, but as they were the other side of the signal box to the target they could not see what the Major was shooting at. They cowered behind a couple of milk churns on the platform. The train passed some trees and soon the station was disappearing from sight. The Major slumped back in the truck feeling dejected that his quarry had escaped. He pulled out a handkerchief and began to give attention to the bloody hole in his jacket sleeve. It wouldn't be until the train stopped at the end of the branch line seven minutes later to unload its ammunition supplies and guns for the army camp at Penhale that the help Cregoe had summoned from the 58th Light Anti-Aircraft Regiment finally got to the Major. But that was seven minutes too late.

Chapter 13

Twenty four hours later the Major was sat in the Colonel's office back in the Depot at Bodmin. His arm was in a sling from the bullet wound received on the train. Fortunately the Infirmary at Truro had said it was just a flesh wound. The bullet had missed the bone, and the Major had been told as long as he kept the wound free of infection he should heal quickly. However, having just arrived back from the hospital, he was in a foul mood as he glared at those stood around the office. The C.O. Colonel Comford was seated behind his desk. Captain Cregoe was seated to the side: next to him the Officer from the Military Police that had the Major had met on Sunday evening. Also present was the Depot's Intelligence Officer and his equivalent from Cregoe's regiment, the Worcesters.

"Who is he? And how is he able to roam across the Cornish countryside and we not able to pick him up?" bellowed the Major.

"According to the signal box man at Shepherd's, he got into a car parked on the road by the farmhouse and drove off after he escaped your clutches on the train," offered Cregoe, the only one daring to speak.

"How long had that been parked there?"

"The signalman believes since early Monday morning. He thinks the gentleman caught the early morning train to Truro."

"Gentleman! He's no gentleman. He's a deadly foe on the loose!" exclaimed the Major not believing his ears. "So how did he know that ammunition train would take him back to his car? It seems no one else knew where the blasted thing was headed from what you tell me of the signalman at Bodmin Road!"

"We think that was just co-incidence. The next passenger train due at Bodmin Road would have gone to Truro from where he could have caught a connection back to Shepherds. However, the passenger train was halted at Doublebois to give priority to the ammunition train. Our man obviously realised we were onto him and just jumped for the fastest escape route available."

"So we know he was in Bodmin on Friday and killed there. We think it was the same killer some time Saturday at Padstow. He then rolls up in a car, catches a train early Monday morning at Shepherds, turns up in Bodmin for a case, shoots your corporal and is calmly waiting for a train at Bodmin Road when we catch up with him. What was in the case? Where is the case? He didn't have a case with him when he jumped onto the train."

"Possibly it contained the weapon he shot you with. If not, then we have no idea," ventured Cregoe.

"So have the railway staff at Shepherds been able to give us any more details?"

"It seems he's used the station three or four times in the past few weeks. Always leaves a car in the lane."

"So where is the car now? Where is he hiding out?"

The Depot Intelligence Officer cleared his throat. "We checked out the Toldish Tunnel that you mentioned to Captain Cregoe. There's nothing there except a few rats, sir."

"So has the woman in St Nicholas Street been able to tell us anymore? And what about her daughter? Has anyone spoken to her yet?"

"We were just about to do that, Major, when we got word you were on your way back from Truro," answered Cregoe.

"Good, I'll come with you when we finish here. And have we kept this from the local newspaper bods? The last thing we want is the public frightened to death by reports of some enemy agent or fifth columnist roaming at will."

"Yes, I've sat on that one," said the Colonel. "And we've hit the railway employees with the Official Secrets Act as well. Section 2 works quite nicely there!"

"So who is this fellow?" The Major's voice sounded really vexed. "The woman in St Nicholas Street said he was Dutch. Is he? He seems to know his way around this part of Cornwall very well for a refugee who's just escaped the claws of the Nazis. Is he one of ours, or one of theirs? Is he a traitor or an enemy? It's no good building defences against an invasion if we can't deal with the ones already here!"

The Worcesters' Intelligence Officer spoke for the first time. "We believe the bullet used to shoot our man on Monday morning was German. The surgeon was able to remove it from the corporal's abdomen. However, given the chaos on the continent recently it's possible it could have come across the Channel with anyone. We can't tell when it was manufactured, so it could even have been here from before the war."

"Is your man alright?" asked the Major grateful that his own wound wasn't worse.

"He'll be in hospital for a while, but the doctor expects him to make a good recovery."

The Major gave a sigh of relief. He knew they could have been looking at more than just the two killed thus far. His anger had dissipated. He was now ready for action again.

The Colonel spoke. "We have put out an alert to all troops in mid Cornwall to be on the look-out. He is bound to show his hand again and then we'll have him."

"Well, gentlemen," said the Major. "Please keep me informed of all developments. I shall have to keep London briefed. Be vigilant and we'll get him. I think we are finished here." He stood up. "Captain, who's coming to St Nicholas Street?"

―――――――――

The trio stood on the pavement looking at the house in St Nicholas Street. It had been agreed that the Major and Captain Cregoe would interview the woman and her daughter while the Military Police officer would talk to his men who had been posted on the house to see if they had picked up anything from the overheard conversations or the comings and goings at the house.

The door was opened by a Military Policeman. He saluted and then acknowledged his officer.

"Mr Johns is here, sir," he said giving the first news of the arrival of the man of the house. He showed them into the front room. The couple stood as the deputation appeared round the door.

"Don't get up," the Major said. His instruction was ignored. The polite gesture impressed the Major. Mrs Johns' eyes widened as she took in the fact that he had been injured since she last saw him. "Mr Johns, I presume," he added, stretching out his good arm to shake the RAF man's hand.

"Yes sir, Harry Johns." His handshake was firm. "My C.O. has given me twenty four hour compassionate leave just to come and check on the missus. Dreadful goings on." He indicated an empty sofa for the Major and Captain to sit on and all were seated. The Military Police Officer had stayed out in the hallway to talk with his two men. He'd kept a presence there since the events of Friday, the six policemen doing four hours on, eight hours off.

The Major opened the questioning. "Your guest is proving quite elusive, Mrs Johns. We want you to tell us again everything you know about this Johann from the moment he first arrived asking for a room right up to when you last saw him on Friday."

Mrs Johns took a deep breath. Her husband nodded. He thought he might get a coherent tale now. In the hour since he'd arrived on his bicycle all he'd got were dramatic snippets interspersed with his wife's sobs. The cup of tea he'd made her stood cold in the cup.

The presence of her husband seemed to fortify Mrs John's as she elucidated the tale of the Dutchman's arrival just over a fortnight before. She related how she couldn't understand, let alone pronounce, his surname so he'd told her to call him Johann. She said he didn't have much with him, but you wouldn't expect a refugee to have an abundance of possessions, although he seemed to have money as he paid her a week in advance. Apart from picking up a few more details on the clothes he wore and the fact that he had left train tickets for Truro in a shirt pocket he had asked Mrs Johns to wash at the beginning of last week the Major and the Captain gleaned nothing new.

"Is your daughter at work?" the Captain asked.

"No, it's her morning off," Mrs John's replied. "Just as well what with Harry coming home. She went to her room when I got a bit upset earlier and Harry made me a cup of tea which I still haven't drunk. Sorry Harry, love." She patted her husband arm as a sign of apology. "Would you like me to call her?" she asked the officers.

"Yes please," said the Captain.

"And we'd be grateful if we could have a word with her alone, if you don't mind," the Major added.

Mrs Johns opened her mouth to speak but her husband got in first.

"Give her a call, and then I'll boil the kettle again and make you a fresh cup of tea. Perhaps the officers would like one too."

"That would be much appreciated," replied the Major. The airman shooed his wife out the door.

The Major and the Captain exchanged glances but said nothing as they waited. There was a knock on the door and a young woman appeared. The twenty two year old was attractive. She was short, just five foot five. She had a good head of short wavy black hair, a rounded face and was wearing a touch of lipstick that accentuated the redness of her lips. She was wearing a tight jumper that showed off the ample contours of her womanhood, and a knee length skirt. It was obvious why the soldiers would be falling over themselves to have this young woman on their arm.

"Mother said you wanted to speak with me," she said in a strong Cornish accent. The Major made the introductions and said, "Kara, We would like you to tell us all you can remember about Johann."

"Mother thinks he done the murder, but he wouldn't hurt anyone," she blurted instantly going on the defensive."

"I beg to differ," said the Major raising his arm in the sling. "But let's not make judgements, we want facts, details. When did you first see him, speak to him, that kind of thing?"

Kara blushed. "The first time I saw him and spoke to him was the day after he arrived. I was coming down the stairs and he was stood at the bottom. He watched me walk down and then as I passed him he said 'You've got beautiful legs!' And I told him 'You've got a cheek!' But he just laughed 'You take not a compliment.' I replied, 'I might if it's genuine.'"

She continued, "We spoke whenever we passed after that. I think he was a bit lonely. Not surprising mind, him being a refugee and all. He told me he came to Falmouth by sea."

"Did he say in which ship?" the Major asked.

"No he just said it was a little boat."

"How did he come to Bodmin?" the Major probed.

"By train," she replied. "He said he had got a job that involved him travelling around a bit on the railways and that Bodmin was a good place to be as you can go north, south, east and west reasonably easily from Bodmin."

"Did he say what his job was?" the Captain interjected.

"No, he said it was better I didn't know. So I took from that he was doing something for the war. You don't like to ask too many questions. You know what the posters say 'Be like Dad – keep Mum!'"

"Do you know any of the places he went to?" asked the Major hoping for a nugget that could prove helpful.

"He said he'd been to Wadebridge, to Padstow, to Fowey and Truro. Oh, and he once said what a windy station Water Chase was."

The Captain looked at the Major blankly. The name meant nothing to him. The Major laughed. "I think he meant Chacewater, where you change for the Perranporth line.

"Oh I think I've heard of it, but I've never been to Perranporth," Kara's expression was as blank as the Captain's, that part of Cornwall was as foreign to her as it was to him.

"Did he ever say anything about meeting anyone?" asked the Major.

"No, I can't recall him saying that. He seemed more interested in places than people."

"What makes you say that?"

"I just remember one occasion where he was fussing over a train timetable saying he had to get somewhere the next day. He was talking about whether to get there by going to Truro or by going to Newquay. Don't ask me where it was, I haven't a clue, but he was comparing train times."

The Major and the Captain looked at each other. "Shepherds," they said together.

"No, I don't think he was a farmer. His hands were too smooth." Kara was trying to be helpful but unaware they were talking of a place rather than an occupation. They didn't enlighten her.

"Did he ever take anything with him? Did he have a case or a bag of any sort?" This time it was the Captain who posed the question.

"I didn't see him come and go every day but I can't remember seeing him carrying anything."

"Are you sure?"

"The only case I can recollect was the small briefcase he kept under the bed. He got upset once because mother had moved it when she cleaned his room."

"What was it like? Did you ever see what was in it?"

"No, Mother doesn't like me going in the guest's rooms. I think she said it was black, but you'll have to ask her to be sure."

The Major took over the questioning again. "Your mother says you walked out with Johann on a couple of occasions. Can you tell us about those times?"

Kara blushed. "What is there to tell? He asked me to go for a walk with him one evening, which I did."

"Where did you go?"

"We walked down the road towards Lostwithiel, and then up the lane towards Carminnow Cross and then back along Castle Road."

The Major turned to the Captain. "That's a stroll around the Barracks by the sounds of it." He turned back to the young woman.

"If it's not too personal a question, miss, may I ask what you did on this walk?"

"Just walked and talked. What kind of young lady do you think I am?" Kara said indignantly.

"I am not suggesting you did anything improper, miss. We just need to build up as detailed a picture as possible of what this young man's activities were."

"He did kiss me for the first time on the walk," proffered Kara feeling a little embarrassed to be confessing the intimate details of her perambulation with these two officers.

"We're not interested in that kind of thing miss," said the Major.

"Wait," said the Captain, his old detective nose sensing there was more to this. "Where did this kiss happen?"

"As we were coming back down by the barracks. There's a gate up by the lane that leads to Coldharbour Farm. He had just taken my picture when two soldiers came out through the gate, so he swept me into his arms and kissed me."

"Taken your picture!" The Major was dumbfounded. "You mean a photograph with a camera?"

"No he set up his easel and painted my portrait! What do you think? Of course, with a camera."

The Major smiled. His response had asked for the sarcasm. "You realise there are regulations that deal with taking pictures. He asked you to pose with a military building in the background."

"I hadn't thought of it like that. I'm not in trouble, am I?" asked the young woman, concern now etched all over her face.

"You're not, but he most certainly could be," the Major responded.

"Did he take any other photographs?" the Captain interjected.

Kara thought for a minute. "Two more," she said. "One when we were on the railway bridge on the lane up to the Cross. That was the first. He said he'd like a picture to remember me by. The second was on Castle Road. He said he was taking a view of the Beacon."

"What kind of camera did he have?" asked the Captain.

"I don't know. I don't know much about cameras. It was small. I'd never seen one that small before. It had a name engraved on the top, you know, the make."

"Voigtlander," suggested the Captain.

"No, it wasn't a big name like that. I think it began with an L, but I couldn't be sure."

"Leica," said the Major.

"It could be, but I can't be certain."

"Sounds likely," said the Major looking towards the Captain. "When the Schleswig-Holstein crew visited Falmouth in 1938 they all seemed to have Leica cameras and were happily snapping away."

"Grief," said the Captain. "Aren't they the crew that came to the Barracks and played a football match?"

"Not in 1938. The only football match they played then was against the dock workers in Falmouth," explained the Major.

"No, one of the Depot men was telling me. This was last year, March I think he said. They all did the Hitler salute when they lined up at kick-off."

"I'd left Bodmin by then," the Major said. "Perhaps they didn't get all the reconnaissance photographs they wanted on that occasion."

"Did you ever see the photographs? Did he have them developed?" asked the Captain turning attention back once more to the bemused young woman.

"No, I never. Perhaps he hasn't finished the roll of film. No, sorry. I haven't seen the camera from that day to this."

"Not to worry, you've been most helpful," reassured the Major.

"I haven't got him into trouble, have I?" said Kara suddenly sensing she had probably said too much.

"No," smiled the Captain, "a few photographs are the least of our concerns."

"And me, you're not going to have me arrested, are you?"

"No, certainly not while you keep answering our questions," the Captain smiled. Kara gave a wan smile not certain that there wasn't a veiled threat in his reply.

"So you went for a walk on that occasion. When else did you see Johann?" asked the Major.

"He had a meal with Mother and myself one day. The other men usually have their food at the barracks, so I felt sorry for him and asked if he could come to tea. Mother doesn't usually do meals for the lodgers. She eventually gave in and he joined us one day. He even helped with the washing up and stayed chatting long into the evening."

"He didn't say anything about his work, or about where he came from?"

"No, I can't recall he did. He did say he enjoyed the lake and mountains as a boy but didn't say…"

"That didn't strike you as strange?" the Major interrupted.

"Strange, no. We were all talking about childhood memories." Kara looked from one to the other bemused as to what could possibly be strange.

"And he said he was from the Netherlands?"

"Yes, that's what he told Mother." Kara was none the wiser.

The two officers nodded to each other but ventured no explanation.

"Are there any other occasions you spent time with this young man?" the Major asked.

"The only other occasion was when he took me for a drive in his car," Kara answered.

"Car?" repeated the Major.

"Well, it wasn't a pony and trap, put it that way." Kara's sarcasm had returned. "We didn't feed it hay or carrots, if that's what you want to know." She sensed that her questioner was uncomfortable at having fallen once more. She pressed her advantage. "We did have to feed it petrol…"

"Where did you buy the petrol?" the Captain was in like a shot.

Kara squirmed in her seat. Her advantage had not lasted long. The Captain sensed her unease.

"It wasn't from an ordinary garage, was it?" he asked.

Kara realised she was cornered. "No," she said looking at her lap.

"Where was it?"

"It was some farm up the Moor road," she said. "I don't know what it was called. It was dark. The farmer sold him some from a shed in the yard."

"Did you recognise the farmer?" the Captain pressed.

"Yes, that was the trouble, see. He sometimes comes into the Hotel where I work. I was shrinking down in my seat hoping he wouldn't see me. I didn't want him telling my boss and my mother getting to hear of it."

"His name?"

"You won't tell him it's me who told you, will you?"

"Me tell him, never," said the Captain leaving open the possibility of someone else doing that.

Kara gave the details of the customer of the Royal Hotel which the Captain duly entered in the notebook he'd taken from his pocket.

"You said it was dark. It must have been late. Where were you going?" the Major continued the interrogation.

"I don't know. We drove back through town and went down to Respryn but after that I was lost. Lots of little lanes. They all look the same to me, especially in the dark. And I wasn't there for the scenery."

"Meaning?" the Major sought clarification.

"Well, don't tell my Mother this but I was hoping he might kiss me again, so I wasn't taking too much notice of where he was driving me."

"So did you go anywhere, or just drive through the lanes?" asked the Major unsure of how he'd phrased the question.

"We did stop. I don't know where. It was pitch dark. He said he had to do something and left me in the car. He took something out the boot and left me. He was gone for what seemed like ages. I don't have a watch but it must have been a good half hour or more. Then all of a sudden I hear the boot being opened and he's back again. I went to tell him what I thought of being left but that's when he kissed me again and I never did get to reprimand him."

"And you don't know where this was?"

"I've told you, it was dark. And besides, they have been removing all the signposts round here. How was I supposed to know?"

"What did your mother say when you got back?"

"I don't think she knew what time we got back."

"Where did he park the car?"

"Over at the station."

"Did you ever see him use the car on any other occasion?" the Captain picked up the questioning. There was a pause.

"Come to think of it, I don't believe I did," Kara said thoughtfully. "Like I've said, he usually went to work on the trains."

"Was the car still at the station the following day?"

"No, it had gone," she replied. "I remember noticing that as I went out to work. But Mum had said Johann had left early that morning, so I assume he took it."

"Was the car his? Or had he a loan of it from someone else?"

"I don't know. He didn't say."

"Doesn't it seem odd that someone who is a refugee suddenly turns up with a car?"

"Not if you are trying to impress a young lady," came the retort. "I've had that happen to me before. It's amazing what lengths those soldiers at the barracks will go to in order to get a lass to themselves."

"And you normally go for late night drives with whichever young man pitches up with a car?"

"What you implying, mister?" Kara sounded annoyed at the line the Captain's questions were taking. She looked as if she was going to say more, but there was a knock at the door and her father brought in a tray of teacups and put them down on the small table. It brought the interview to an end.

Twenty minutes later after an exchange of small talk over a cup of tea the officers were back outside in St Nicholas Street walking towards the Barracks.

"I can't but help thinking the daughter wasn't telling us all she knows," said the Major.

"I think she's too taken up with having a good time with the young men who've suddenly arrived in her life to be much more use to us," replied the Captain. "Why do you think she knows where she went that night?"

"I'm not sure. It will be worth us tracking down this farmer that's selling petrol. That's got to be the black market."

"Isn't that a job for the local constabulary?" asked the Military Policeman.

"After we've had a word first," said the Major. "We'll see what the farmer can tell us about his customer before the boys in blue bring him in front of the magistrate."

The Major's attention was distracted by a couple up on the station forecourt. It was on a higher level than the street separated by a low wall but from their side of the road the Major had a good view of the front entrance of the station. A pretty young woman in uniform was embracing a young soldier who hugged her, swept her off her feet, and spun her round. When he put her down again she was laughing, obviously delighted to see this young fellow. His arms held onto hers as they spoke although they were too far away to be heard. The Major's stomach tightened. He recognised the uniform – its wearer was a member of the ATS. Not unusual as there were a growing number of them now based at the Depot, but the poise, the hair, the… - it was Elizabeth. He thought back to that kiss in the carriage on the train on Monday morning. Perhaps it had meant nothing. Perhaps he had read too much into it. Perhaps he was hoping where there was no aspiration to be had. She was a beautiful lady and he had no claim on her. But hadn't she kissed his cheek first? Who was this young man to make him feel the pangs of jealousy? In Padstow he felt she was still grieving the loss of her fiancé, but the embrace he had just witnessed seemed so heartfelt. She obviously knew this soldier, was pleased at their meeting. The Major shook his head trying to assuage the sadness that was sweeping over him. He felt a sense of loss, but couldn't rationalise it. He had never experienced such pangs of emotion before. He had only known Elizabeth a few days. He glanced across again but the angle of the wall now hid them from sight.

"Didn't you hear me?" said the Captain.

"Er, no. What did you say?" asked the Major suddenly awakened from his own train of thought.

The Captain repeated his offer of a meal at the Officer's Mess. The Major accepted although he felt as if his appetite had just vanished. The trio walked round the Great War Memorial and into the Keep

Chapter 14

The Captain slowed the Major's Humber Snipe as he turned off the metalled road onto the farm track. He felt very honoured to be driving such a vehicle. It was over their meal the Major had suggested they retrieve the car from the Bodmin North Station and then take a drive out to the farm. It was the Depot cook who had told them where they would find the farmer. He seemed to know many of the farmers round about buying direct from them to feed the hungry troops. The Major winced at every bump on the rough track as his good arm helped cradle the wounded arm in its sling. The track mounted a slight rise before dropping down past an old quarry and they pulled up at Callabarrett Farm. It didn't look much of a farm. There was the farmhouse which was more of a cottage than a house. There were a couple of lean to sheds on either side of the cottage and a low linhay. An ancient looking lorry was parked by the quarry. The Captain stopped the car on the track and the two men got out.

As the Major rounded the front of the car he was greeted by the bark of a scruffy looking border collie. By the looks of him he was a working dog used to the delights of moorland weather. The Major spoke gently to reassure him as he joined the Captain.

"Let's have a look in the barn before we knock the door," the Major said nodding across towards the linhay. The dog had stopped his barking and now followed them. There was the usual scattering of farm implements and the officers wove their way round them to the open-fronted barn. On one side were wooden shelves covered in tins of nails and jars with screws in and tools. On the other side a greasy tarpaulin covered a mound. The Captain lifted a corner. There must have been a half a dozen petrol cans. The four gallon rectangular containers were made of pressed steel.

The Captain let out a low whistle. "These are army flimsies. He must be using army fuel."

"That explains the remains of brown soggy bread on the floor then," replied the Major. The Captain looked puzzled.

"It's how they remove the red dye in army petrol. They try to filter the fuel through the bread to remove the dye. Then they can sell it on the black market," the Major explained. The dog turned and ran out of the linhay. The officers turned to see what had distracted him.

Approaching them with a lop-sided gait was a man in a flat cap, probably about fifty, dressed in an old jacket, dark trousers and wellington boots.

"What yer looking fur?" he said as he got closer. "There's nuffing in there for the likes of ye."

The Major ascertained he was the farmer they were seeking and raised the issue of his 'customers'.

"That's my ration for the farm. I have a tractor and my lorry. I don't know anything about customers," said the farmer.

"Those are nice new petrol cans. Army issue. So let's talk about your supplier, then," said the Captain turning back and lifting the whole tarpaulin off the stockpile.

"I accept they'm army cans," the farmer replied. "I got them off the Depot in Bodmin. I'm old DCLI, y'see. That's where I copped this one," he explained as he pointed down to his leg. "Doing my bit for King and Country the last time we had to fight them there Jerrymans."

"It's not just the cans that are army, but the fuel as well," said the Captain as he picked a can up and held it high in one hand. With the other he swung it on its little handle so he could see the bottom. There was a clear WD 1940 on the bottom along with the manufacturer's initials. He put the half empty can down on the ground and began to unscrew its top. He tilted it over until some of the fuel poured out onto the ground. It was a red colour.

"Don't go wasting my ration," said the farmer somewhat put out at this careless use of his precious commodity.

"Your ration or your black market supply?" asked the Major. "Either you start telling us about the 'customer' we want to know about or we'll be taking your little supply here right off your hands this very minute."

Cornered as he was, the farmer felt he had little option but to reveal the details of his transaction. The officers learned little other than their man was driving a black Ford Eight, a nice compact little car that would have cost £100 new before the war, but was feared by many for its lack of brakes. Their man had paid cash for his petrol.

As the Captain turned the car and the two officers drove up the track, the farmer stood ruffling his dog's head, grateful that the two army men had not carried out their threat to remove his supply of petrol. Little did he know that after visiting the roadblock just a little further up the A30 on the rise before the road dipped down to Cardinham Lodge to see if the men there were aware of any night time comings and goings to the farm, they would stop at the police station on their way down the hill into Bodmin and report his black market activities to the wide-eyed sergeant at the desk. By the following morning his supply would be gone, and he and two soldiers from the Depot would soon be appearing before the police courts.

It was a fine and clear morning with just a light breeze as the Humber Snipe drove out of the East Gate of the Barracks. The Captain smiled to himself at again being able to drive this beauty. The Major had pulled the strings with General Comford to get the Captain to act as his driver for the journey to Pendennis Castle in Falmouth. The Major had a meeting that afternoon to assess the readiness of the Category A port's defences, and while the Major's assessment would be based on the reports those in command would provide, he had suggested to the General the Captain could usefully have a look at the line of pillboxes that were hastily being constructed to defend the port from a landward attack. The fear was of a landing on one or more of the beaches either side of the Fal estuary then circling round to put the large coastal guns at Pendennis Castle and St Anthony Head out of action leaving the port vulnerable to a seaborne invasion. It was a tactic that had been successfully used against St Mawes Castle in the Civil War in the seventeenth century when it surrendered to the Parliamentarian forces on the hill behind without firing a shot because all its cannon pointed seaward. The Major was also keen to have someone he trusted having a look at what was on the ground rather than the rose-tinted view he was likely to receive from those who may try to tell him what they thought he wanted to hear.

It had been a pleasant drive down the A30 and then off at Fraddon down the Tresillian Valley towards Truro. They had stopped at the Wheel Inn in Tresillian for a delightful lunch. Apart from a handful of regulars, mainly old men, being curious as to why these officers should stop in their village, one would not have known the country was at war. The thatched 14th century inn had seen activity in the Civil War. The landlord had taken great delight in telling his visitors that the Roundhead Commander Thomas Fairfax had had his headquarters in the inn during the negotiations with the Royalist Hopton over Truro in 1645 and even claimed a notch in the table at which they were sat came from a careless Cavalier sword. Now feeling full from their lunch, the Captain was driving alongside the creek into the village of Perranworthal. He was impressed at the ease with which the car pulled up the winding hill before the Major told him to take a left to drop down into Penryn. After passing the laundry in the Praze and a long street of warehouses and stores they finally emerged at the bridge and the riverside.

"Slow down a little," the Major said. "I don't want to miss anything as we drive into the town." The Captain eased down to twenty five as the gasworks came into view. There against the embankment was a flurry of activity as soldiers stripped to their waist were cementing the concrete blocks on a pillbox that was rapidly taking shape.

"Good field of fire covering the approach road," commented the Major. "A well-chosen site."

"But what's that behind?" asked the Captain leaning forward to get a clearer view. "Grief, it's a graveyard!"

"That's the Jewish Cemetery," replied the Major. "Though there is a Dissenter's Burial ground next door, I believe."

"The relatives won't like a pillbox next to their loved ones graves, but needs must, I suppose," said the Captain.

"I don't think there's been a burial in the Jewish cemetery for over twenty five years. Oh, we need to fork left here." The Major interrupted the discussion to give directions.

The road passed a few cottages and a meadow before bending round to hug the line of the river on its way down to Falmouth. They had just begun to curve round to the right when the sound of an aeroplane could be heard. The Major glanced to his left. There coming down the Penryn river at quite a height was a German plane, its black crosses clearly visible for all to see.

"Heinkel," shouted the Major. The Captain acted instinctively swerving into an opening on his left bringing the car to a sudden stop under the shade of a tree. Both men jumped out and knelt by the car their eyes skyward following the flight of the bomber. Both had experienced the strafing bombing runs of the Luftwaffe during the retreat in Belgium and France and this was bringing back the memories of roads clogged with cart pushing refugees as dive bombers machine-gunned all and sundry not discriminating between soldier and civilian, combatant and child before dropping their deadly explosives.

"He's after the docks," said the Major. Both men stood and moved to the hedge as they saw the bombs begin to fall from the belly of the machine as it dived towards its target. The bomb aimer had miscalculated. The bombs fell beyond the village of Flushing on the opposite side of the Penryn river on the wooded headland at Trefusis and a couple dropped in the water.

"Four hundred yards short," the Major estimated.

"There's another one," exclaimed the Captain. Sure enough, just a couple of seconds behind the first was a second bomber, again on a course down the Penryn river and diving for the docks.

This time the aim was accurate. The stick of bombs fell across the vessels at the Northern Arm of the Docks. One seemed to go down the funnel of one of the steamers. There were explosions, and very quickly it could be seen that there were several fires as well. The anti-aircraft guns on a Dutch naval vessel moored in the harbour opened up on the fleeing bombers as they made off across the bay to the south east. From the docks a big thick black column of smoke began to spiral heavenwards blighting the blue sky on this warm, summer's day.

The Major crossed the road and climbed the steps onto the raised pavement in order to get a better view. The Captain followed. In silence they watched as the fires seemed to be spreading from the two ships on the inside of the arm, across the wharf itself and onto the ships on the outside of the arm. Soon the flames and smoke became one conflagration so it was impossible to tell what was ship and what was dock.

A handful of soldiers emerged from the lane that the Captain had blocked as he had screeched the car to a halt.

"Jerry back again," said one as he looked across to the Docks. They stood looking for a minute or two before the sergeant said, "Right back to work. That anti-tank block is not going to build itself, and it seems it's going to be needed sooner than most people think."

The Major watched them saunter back down the lane towards the Boyer's Cellars wharf thinking he'd inspect their work on their way back.

"Look," said the Captain bringing the Major's attention back to the Docks.

"What is it?" asked the Major.

"There on the end. There seems to be a whole group of men on the end of the wharf," said the Captain in horrified tones. Sure enough there seemed to be a mass of humanity on the stone section of the wharf at the end of the arm. Their escape route was cut off by the fire.

The Major made his way back to the car, went rummaging in the glove box and soon returned to the Captain with a pair of binoculars and a camera. Behind them a few people were emerging from their homes to look at the scene across the water. The Captain took the binoculars and began to survey the inferno. The Major, as best he could with his one good arm, held the Argus camera to his face and peered through the viewfinder. He took several photographs of the column of smoke before being interrupted by the Captain who began giving a commentary on the detail he was making out.

"It's the SS Tiara on the outside of the dock. She's a petroleum tanker by the looks of it. No wonder she's burning. The one next to her seems to be burning fore and aft. I can't see the stern of the two ships the other side of the wharf. The flames and smoke are terrific. There are men in the water."

"Probably jumped to escape the fires," suggested the Major.

"There's a launch coming to pick them up." In fact small boats seemed to be converging on the Northern Arm from several directions. A couple of tugs were pulling an undamaged tanker away towards Trefusis Point. Other vessels seemed to be headed for the end of the wharf where the crowd of men had congregated.

"There was no siren warning." The voice came from a white haired man who had ventured down his garden path and joined the officers on the pavement.

"Really?" the Captain responded more in exclamation than question.

"Same as Monday. Then the siren went off after the bombs hit the water."

"How many raids you had, then?" asked the Captain.

"This is the eighth since Friday," the man replied. "They keep going for the docks, although on Sunday they killed a family up in town. Lister Street they say was hit quite bad. Poor souls. Don't know how many will be killed in that lot." He nodded towards the docks. The smoke was now considerable and reaching to quite a height.

From behind them came the sound of a clanging bell and a roaring engine. They all turned to see the Penryn fire engine driving at speed towards them.

"We'd better get going," said the Major and the two officers returned to the car and drove on past the Greenbank Hotel and down High Street into the town centre. They made their way up past the church and it wasn't until they emerged waterside beyond Taylor's Garage that they could see the huge size and thickness of the plume of smoke. Here people were stood all along the railing towards the Admiralty Pier quietly watching.

"Should we go to the Docks and see if we can help?" asked the Captain.

"What can I do?" replied the Major lifting his arm in the sling. "There'll be plenty of men in the docks who know the place who will be doing that. We'd only get in the way. If the Penryn fire brigade have arrived, you can be sure the Falmouth one is there as well as the Docks own fire crew. No keep going."

The Captain drove on past the Killigrew monument and into Bar Road. He pulled in to allow an ambulance to overtake him, and another car following went by as well.

"What's that idiot doing chasing the ambulance at a time like this?" asked the Captain.

"Didn't you see the markings on the door? That's a car for sitting cases. It keeps the ambulance free for the seriously injured."

"Oh right, I'll let him off then," said the Captain as he drove on. They rounded the corner by the entrance to the docks where a small group of concerned women had already gathered, probably desperate to check that their husband or son was not among the casualties. They drove under the railway arch and over the crossroads. As the road began to rise they were brought to a halt at a roadblock. Having explained their business and shown their papers they were allowed through.

"Tell you what," said the Major. "Take a left here. Instead of driving straight on towards the castle we'll go up the hill and have a look at the docks from there."

The Captain swung the car onto Castle Drive and continued up the hill.

"Get past the fields here, then just beyond those trees, stop. We should get a good view between the trees down onto the Docks and the Station."

The Captain pulled up as instructed and the two men got out of the car. Between two trees growing on the low hedge to a short sloping field, they were given a grandstand view of the Docks. They were now able to see the Northern Arm from the other side. Here they could see the frantic efforts to rescue the men from the two ships on this side of the Wharf. There were fires both fore and aft on the two ships. Some rope ladders hung over the side. There were a couple of small launches picking men from the water. They had decided to jump rather than face the raging inferno on the ships behind them. One of the burning vessels was well down to its stern.

"Looks as if that one's sinking," said the Captain as they sought to make sense of the scene unfolding before them. A couple of launches were alongside the end of the wharf. Someone at the end of the Wharf was directing the men who were descending a ladder onto the deck of the boats. Those who were being brought forward were stooping with their shoulders wide and their arms hanging.

"They must be burned something awful," said the Major thinking aloud. "They seem to be taking off the wounded first." He was amazed that even in the midst of such devastation there was a semblance of order. As one boat was full, its deck covered with men, it pulled away and the next one came in to continue the rescue. The boat headed across the harbour towards the Custom House Quay. There, as the boat neared, an ambulance appeared, the crowd on the Quay parting to let it through. However, back on the vessels that had been bombed and were still burning fiercely, it looked as if it had been every man for himself. The Major watched as several sets of willing hands grabbed another person in the water and hauled him onto one of the small boats circling around between the wharf and the shore. Some of them must have been in the water for twenty minutes or more, maybe thirty. From their vantage point, he could see the firemen bringing up yet another pump to combat the fires which were raging unabated.

"A couple of those are tankers, and even if they are empty the fumes will burn," he said to the Captain who had stood transfixed at the horror of the searing, devouring blaze beneath them.

"It's Rotterdam all over again," is all he said. Then after a pause he added, "Well it would be if it was more than just two planes. Thank God that's all that came."

"But like Rotterdam, where are the anti-aircraft guns? If this is a Category A port, to be defended at all costs, Falmouth has to have anti-aircraft cover," said the Major sounding angry. "The newspaper report on Sunday's raid said the AA guns were in action, but they can only mean those on the ships. In fact I think that will be my first question at this afternoon's meeting," he added. "Come on, I've seen enough here. Let's go and kick them into action before Jerry gets here in a big way."

The officers returned to the car.

"Instead of turning round to take the short route to the Castle, let's carry on round Castle Drive and see what we can see of the defences they are preparing." The Major was keen to have a feel for how things were on the ground before he went into his meeting. They drove down to Pendennis Point and got out of the car.

"Well, that's an improvement on the wooden hut that was here when I last visited," said the Major pointing to a concrete structure down towards the searchlight that served the Half Moon Battery. Down on the shoreline a platoon were battling with coils of barbed wire that they were fixing to prevent anyone scrambling ashore on the rocks of the point below the searchlight. He turned to look back at the Castle. The original gun tower built by Henry VIII was clearly visible on the top of the peninsula. Below it on the slopes hidden amongst camouflage netting were two guns.

"The Munich Crisis made them decide they needed to reinstate the guns here. However the old mountings were no good so they had to completely re-dig the gun pits. This is the first time I've seen the new guns in place," said the Major.

"They are still vulnerable to strafing from the air," responded the Captain studying the battery up on the hill. "They need to be enclosed in gun houses. That was one of our problems in France. Jerry strafes from the air before he sends in the ground troops."

"Thanks, I'll raise it at the meeting. Talking of which it's almost time." They drove along the west side of the headland. There in the woods were more troops digging some defence posts. When finished they would be two man slit trenches allowing the soldiers with rifles or perhaps a Bren gun to cover the approach to the woods and the Castle. The Captain turned sharply to go up the Castle drive. Partway up were four men already in post with a Spigot Mortar. They indicated the car should stop and two men covered as a third approached the car. Business was stated, papers checked and the car was waved through. This was repeated at the Guardhouse just beyond the old drawbridge before the Captain drove into the Castle compound. The place appeared a hive of activity with gunners and engineers everywhere. The column of acrid black smoke rising above the roof of the Castle barracks continued to swell from the inferno at the docks. By the time the Major had confirmed arrangements with the Captain for picking him up later, a Sergeant had appeared all set to take the Major to his meeting.

Chapter 15

Three hours later the Captain was driving a rather exacerbated Major back to Bodmin. "They are still trying to prepare last war defences," he moaned. "Why can't the Generals see that the enemy's tactics have moved on? Take Pendennis itself. They are all about coastal defence. Big guns to defend the harbour. They fail to realise that the biggest threat to them will come from the air."

The Captain looked across at his animated passenger. He decided it was not time to say anything. The Major continued.

"I asked to see their anti-aircraft defences. They showed me two Lewis guns that they've constructed mountings for and that's it! The guns they had scrounged off ships that had returned from France last month. If it wasn't for the Dutch Navy in the harbour those Jerry planes this afternoon would have had an unopposed run at the Docks this afternoon. The Castle didn't fire a shot!"

"If Falmouth's such an important port where are the Heavy Anti-Aircraft guns?" the Captain dared to ask.

"Still being built. I grant they seem to be working flat out on the construction of various gun sites around the estuary but the first ones won't be ready until the end of the month."

"Will Jerry wait that long?"

"That's exactly what I asked them. We are desperately playing for time here, trying to catch up on what should have been done during peace time. Anyway, how did you get on?"

"Better than you by the sounds of it. I drove along the lane that forms the defensive line to the rear of the port. Most of the pillboxes are constructed. I stopped and chatted to some of the Fusiliers who have been brought down to defend this stretch of coast. They seem to know what they're about. I saw eleven pillboxes, nine of them complete. Apparently there's one in a field near the railway on the Penryn side of town I didn't see, plus the one we drove past on the road in. Oh, and I didn't see one on some headland out near where they are building one of those HAA batteries that you spoke about. So that's fourteen along the defensive line. They were working on some anti-tank ditches in some of the fields as well."

"At least that sounds better, but then static defence is something the Generals understand well," said the Major.

"One group told me they had been building some on a beach as well at Swannypool or some such place," the Captain added.

"Yes Swanpool," the Major corrected. "It's a possible landing site." The Major sighed and thought for a moment.

"I have to hand it to Churchill. I think his strategy of a fixed line at the coast to . repel the invader as best we can, backed up by mobile reserves that can be used to plug the places where Jerry breaks through the line, is the right one. He's a canny old fox."

"So is that the lesson from this afternoon for my work on the Bodmin Stop Line?" asked the Captain.

For the rest of the journey the conversation turned to pillboxes at Daymer Bay, anti-tank measures to protect the bridge at Wadebridge, road blocks in Bodmin and mining the field behind the Coastal Gun Battery at St Catherine's Castle in Fowey. The miles flew by until they were halted by the Local Defence Volunteers at a roadblock just beyond Indian Queens near to where the A30 crosses over the railway at St Dennis Junction. It was some of the Captain's men who halted them at the next one by the Bodmin Wireless Station at Innis Downs, just before the road twisted down into the village of Lanivet where again it was the LDV who brought their progress to a halt. There were two more roadblocks as they drove back into Bodmin.

"How about something to eat before we go back to the Barracks?" suggested the Major. "Let's stop at the Royal Hotel in the main street. My tab. I've heard the food's good."

"Best suggestion you've made since leaving Falmouth," smiled the Captain.

They negotiated their way through the roadblock and chicane at the Five Ways junction and drove along Higher Bore Street and into Fore Street dropping down the hill past the Methodist Church where a small group of evacuees were playing a game on the steps. The Captain pulled up right outside the front door of the Royal Hotel with its glass and wrought iron canopy stretching out over the pavement. It had started life as Oliver's Hotel until being granted the Royal Stables for the Post in 1847, and although few ever arrived by horse these days it had retained its Royal status. In fact it had been the black out that put paid to its horse drawn taxi that used to meet the trains at the town's two stations. There had been a collision on St Nicholas Street with a car and the horse had to be put down.

Inside the hotel's restaurant the two officers enjoyed a relaxed meal before adjourning to the hotel's bar. Here there were a handful of officers, a couple of commercial travellers and a spattering of locals enjoying an early evening drink. The troops, that is to say the other ranks, tended to favour the Town Arms which was just a little further up the street next to the old meat market. Thus it became rather noticeable when this refined atmosphere was pierced by a young woman's voice becoming louder and louder from a small party sat over in the corner by the window. Both the Captain and the Major had glanced in their direction on several occasions before they realised they recognised the voice. It belonged to a rather inebriated Kara. She had stayed after her shift at the reception desk and enjoyed a drink or two with some of the men in uniform. She had now unsteadily made her way to the bar to get herself another drink as the group she was with had refused to buy her anymore. The barman, sizing up the situation, told her she had had enough and should make her way home. That was when she turned and recognised the Major.

"Oh, it's you, hello," she said trying to focus on the officer in front of her. She turned back to her group and announced "This is the Major who thinks that my Johann killed the man who was found murdered in my mother's house." That certainly grabbed the attention of the five or six men who were sat round a small table in the corner, and they turned to take in the developing scene.

"You are a nasty man, mister Major. My Johann is a gentleman and he wouldn't hurt anyone," the words were slurred as Kara poked a finger at the Major. "You're the nasty one, mister Major. You scared away my Johann. I haven't seen him since... since, er... I can't remember when."

A young lieutenant stood up and tried to coax Kara away. "Come and sit down again, there's a good lass," he said. Then turning to the Major he added, "I'm sorry for this sir. I think the lady's had a little too much to drink."

"The Major doesn't think I'm a good girl. He thinks I'm in league with a nasty foreigner, don't you Major?" Kara's performance now had the attention of everyone in the bar. She was in no mood to return to her seat and continued to address the major in a loud, penetrating voice.

"Have you found my Johann, Major? Did he take you for a ride in his car? He took me for a ride in his car, but I've already told you that. You do remember me telling you, Major?"

"Shall I fetch the Manager, sir?" asked the barman somewhat alarmed at the way Kara was carrying on.

"That won't be necessary, thank you," the Major replied. Then turning to the Captain he said, "Forget having a drink Captain. I think it would be a good move if we took Kara home in the car." The Captain nodded and cancelled his order with the barman.

"That would be a great help," said the lieutenant, somewhat relieved that this embarrassing young woman was being taken off his hands. "I can't say I fancied guiding her home in this state. Would you like me to accompany you, sir?"

"No, that's fine. She lives on the way back to the Barracks and we were about to go anyway. I'll hand her over to her mother, who won't be too pleased to see her like this, I'm sure."

"Thank you, sir. That's very generous. I'm sure she doesn't mean what she said, sir. It's just the liquor talking."

"Just like Thomas Edison said, 'To put alcohol in the human brain is like putting sand in the bearing of an engine!'" the Major replied anxious to bring the scene to a resolution.

The Captain and the Major stood either side of Kara. The Major put his good arm round Kara and the Captain did likewise on the other side.

"Ooo," she squealed. "Are we going to do the Lambeth Walk?" The two men guided her to the door to the stifled laughs and hushed whispers of many in the bar and took her out to the car where with a little difficulty they got her sat in the back seat. The Major sat in the front. The Captain started the engine. Kara's ramblings continued.

"Are you going to take me for a drive? You didn't like it when I told you Johann took me for a drive, and now you are doing the self-same thing yourself."

"We are driving you home Kara," the Major replied firmly.

"Don't take me home. My mother won't like it. I have never come home drunk before. Poor Mother. She's not going to like it."

It was only a minute before the Captain drew up outside Kara's home in St Nicholas Street. The Major got out and opened the door for Kara. She clambered out and as she stepped onto the pavement, she stumbled. The Major steadied her with his good arm. She responded by putting her arm round his back and he began to guide her towards the house. An army truck drove past. The Major was too occupied to see that it was driven by a woman dressed in ATS uniform. Nor did he see the front passenger of the lorry turn to survey the scene on the pavement. It was at just that moment Kara turned and planted a kiss on the Major's cheek.

"You not a nasty man, Major. You are a kind man."

The Major made no comment but steered Kara towards the front door. He knocked, explained the situation to a disgusted Mrs Johns who took Kara from him. He could feel the sharp whip of her tongue as she harangued her daughter as the door closed behind him and he made his way back to the car.

"I shall be grateful for my bed tonight," the Major told the Captain. "It's been quite a day, one way and another."

Chapter 16

Thursday saw a little more cloud than the day before, but there were still good long sunny spells. The Major felt better for his good night's sleep. The pain in his arm was now little more than a dull ache. Unfortunately the Colonel wouldn't release Captain Cregoe for a second day to be the Major's driver. Understandably he insisted his man fulfil his own duties overseeing the defence works in Lostwithiel and choosing the site of a pillbox that was to guard the river downstream at St Winnow. The Colonel said he hoped the Captain would use what he had seen from the Defence Line at Falmouth to good effect, but he couldn't spare such a valuable officer simply to be a glorified chauffeur again. The Major had accepted it without question, thinking it unfair to use his Churchill letter to force the issue but he did say his own duties would be curtailed due to his arm wound preventing him from driving. The Colonel had offered to provide a driver from the ATS pool that was now based at the Depot. The Major had said as long as she drives well that would be fine.

Now he was stood waiting by his parked car at the back of the officer's quarters for his driver to appear. He was gazing at the paintwork thinking the car needed a wash after its excursions along the windy Cornish lanes and roads, when a voice cut through his ruminations.

"Reporting for duty, sir. On the orders of Colonel Cromford."

The Major looked up in amazement as there before him was Elizabeth.

"I didn't know you could drive," he said as he handed her the keys.

"You didn't ask," she said coldly. "I've been driving for years, ever since father got a tractor for the farm." She took the keys, opened the door for him, and then once he was in the passenger seat, shut it with a little more force than he thought was necessary. He had taken the front passenger seat rather than be chauffeur driven sat in the rear. She thought it a little unusual but knew better than to say anything. He watched her as she walked round the bonnet to the driver's door. She looked splendid. His heart beat a little faster at the thought of spending another day in Elizabeth's company, yet she had a stern look on her face, and she didn't look at him as she got into the driver's seat, inserted the key and started the ignition.

"Where to, sir?" she asked matter of factly.

"We need the Liskeard road," he replied. "We can go out the East Gate and back along Castle Road."

She pulled away smoothly, turned just before the indoor rifle range and stopped at the gate for the sentry to raise the barrier, before turning right into the lane that ran behind the high wall of the Depot. No one spoke until they reached the Liskeard road at Carminnow Cross.

"Turn right here," the Major instructed. There was not a vehicle in sight as she took the junction by the old Celtic cross. He was impressed with the way Elizabeth handled the car, and negotiated the bends down the hill to the Glynn valley. He thought about complimenting her but her fixed glare made him doubt it would be appreciated right now. Besides, he wasn't quite sure where he stood with this young lady. The scene at the railway station flashed before him as he remembered that rather warm embrace he had witnessed. Not that he was prepared to give her up – she was too delightful for that - but he'd have to tread gently.

"Just past the bridge there is a turning on the right to the railway station. You can pull in there and stop."

However, Elizabeth had to stop just before the turning. There was a roadblock with a chicane made of dragon's teeth that guarded the junction from both directions. On the right hand side of the road soldiers were unloading breeze blocks from the back of a truck. There were men on the bank cementing and building a pillbox that would guard the river crossing and the access to the station. Papers were produced and then Elizabeth turned into the side road and pulled up.

"I'll only be five minutes here," said the Major as he opened the door with his good hand. "You can drive up to the station. There'll be plenty of room to turn round there."

"Yes sir," came the icy reply. As the Major closed the door, Elizabeth accelerated away with a squeal of tyres that caused the men to look up from their work. A sergeant hurried up to the Major and saluted. The Major acknowledged the salute and told the sergeant to be at his ease.

"I've just come to see how you are getting on."

"Very well, sir. The lorry with the blocks arrived this morning and we will soon have the walls up on the pillbox," explained the sergeant falling in beside the Major. They walked back to the junction from where the Major could survey all that was being done.

"I like the way you've hidden the roadblock in the dip. Coming down the hill from Bodmin it's disguised by the rise of the bridge, and from the Liskeard direction you would be round that bend and committed to the slope before you realised what you had come upon."

"Thank you sir," acknowledged the sergeant, his face glowing with pride. "The pillbox is slightly elevated on the bank, sir, so it has a withering field of fire upon the main road in both directions." The Major looked both ways and nodded.

"Aren't you a little off the Stop Line out here though?" he asked.

"The Colonel wanted all routes from the south of Bodmin covered, sir. He said he wanted to make Bodmin an anti-tank island. That was his phrase, whatever that might be. There's two pillboxes the other side of Lanhydrock House on the Lostwithiel Road. They also cover the entrance to the track that leads down into the valley below the house and to the railway. The track comes out by the station, sir, so we are here covering the other end of it, as well as any approach up the main road."

"But what about the lane that crosses the bridge at Respryn about a mile downstream from here?" the Major asked.

"I understand it will be blown to prevent anything crossing the river there sir. Shame, it seems a nice little spot."

"Let's hope it doesn't come to that then, sergeant. You've got men patrolling the area?"

"No sir, we've looked at the bridge so we know where to place the charges when the time comes, but those LDV chaps are patrolling that bit of river and the railway tunnel just in case the enemy drop some of their parachute troops behind the front line."

The Major looked across the valley to the large house on the hill. Glynn House sat majestically looking down on the valley with the River Fowey flowing on its journey from the heights of Bodmin Moor down to the sea. There was a truck and a flurry of activity going on at the front door, but the distance was too great to see just what.

"What's happening up there sergeant?" asked the Major pointing to the mansion.

"Wrens, sir. They came through the roadblock about an hour ago. Sent down from Plymouth to Lady Vivian's residence."

"But what do the Navy want here? It's a good fifteen miles to the coast!"

"I'd guess dispersal of stores and administration, sir. They've taken over a china clay dry up behind Bodmin Road station as well. And according to my briefing there's navy at Fowey and Padstow harbours and an aerodrome at somewhere called St Merryn. So I'm guessing this is somewhere in the middle on the railway line from Plymouth, sir."

"Yes it makes sense. Just something else to be aware of if the balloon goes up."

The two men turned as the Major's Humber Snipe quietly rolled to a stop back in the lane that led to the station. Elizabeth certainly returned in a more appropriate manner than she'd left.

"Thank you, sergeant. You and your men are doing a grand job. Keep at it. We may soon be depending on what you achieve here. I'll leave you to it. Good day." The Major returned the sergeant's salute and then turned and strode back to the car.

"Next stop Fowey," the Major said as he settled into the passenger seat.

"Do you want to stay this side of the river to Lostwithiel or do you want me to go back to Lanhydrock so we can go down the west side?" Elizabeth asked without looking at him. He couldn't decide whether she was trying to be helpful or awkward.

"Let's go west, then we don't have to go through Lostwithiel itself," he replied in a manner to show his knowledge of the local roads and lanes was as good as hers. Elizabeth eased the car through the roadblock, over the bridge and up the hill. Eventually the Major decided he had to cut the icy chill.

"Well I at least thought you'd be pleased to see me again," he said unsure of what the response would be.

"Maybe," came the uninformative reply.

"What kind of answer is that?" he asked. "After the manner of our departing last time I thought you would be glad to be in my company."

"It's an answer that depends on whether you are delighted to be with me," she explained.

"Of course I am. I didn't know you were going to be my driver until you arrived at the car, but I have to confess I was thrilled it was you."

"Are you? Really?" she probed, looking at him for the first time in the conversation.

"Yes I am. Why on earth wouldn't I be?" he responded somewhat bemused.

"I thought you'd found someone else to take your fancy," she said keeping her eyes on the road.

"What on earth are you talking about?" His voice sounded quite exasperated. He really didn't have a clue as to what she could be alluding.

"You seemed pretty entwined with a woman in St Nicholas Street on Wednesday evening." Elizabeth could feel the jealousy rise up within her as she spoke.

"I, what?" the Major spluttered not sure he could believe what he was hearing.

"Don't deny it. I saw her plant a kiss on you." Elizabeth couldn't help herself from saying it, knowing she'd played her top card.

"Me? If I'm not mistaken it was you having an embrace outside the station on Tuesday." He hadn't intended to say that but it just spilled out as if it were purely natural that attack was the best form of defence.

"You dolt!" she exclaimed. "That was my cousin. He'd been home on a two day leave which they gave him as he'd been wounded at Dunkirk. He's been in hospital for a month and he was given a two day pass before having to report back to his regiment. I just happened to see him on the platform as I was walking down the road and he came out through the booking hall to greet me."

The Major glanced at Elizabeth with a mixture of embarrassment and relief.

"But you still haven't said who the young lady was that you were with on Wednesday?" She was not going to let him off the hook by diverting the conversation on to her.

"Wednesday?" the Major thought out loud. "I went with the Captain to Falmouth. We had a meal at the Royal when we got back." Then the light went on. He laughed.

"What's so funny?" Elizabeth was annoyed at his mirth.

"After the meal we went into the bar for a drink, but Miss Johns was rather drunk, so we took her home to her mother's house in St Nicholas Street. That's what you must have seen. I helped her out the car to the front door."

"But what is she to you?" Elizabeth wasn't sure this explanation had answered all her questions.

"Nothing. She is a witness in the case of the soldier that was murdered last week. She was saying too much in the Hotel so I decided to take her home." The Major glanced at Elizabeth to gauge her reaction. For the first time that morning he saw the faintest hint of a smile on her lips. Nobody said anything for a minute or two. They negotiated their way through the roadblocks at Treffry Gate and Sweetshouse and were driving along the Fowey road just at the spot where it affords magnificent views down across the verdant Fowey valley.

"Pull over a minute," the Major instructed. Elizabeth duly obeyed pulling onto the rough verge at a spot where the road was wider.

"Let's just take in the beauty of this spot for a moment," he said indicating she should join him in getting out of the car.

They stood taking in the glorious vista. The river winding its way below Lostwithiel as it headed for the sea. The valley sides were dark green with the woods that snaked around every creek and inlet. A train whistled somewhere down in

Lostwithiel. Away in the distance the hills of the moor rose to the horizon hazy in the heat of the summer's day.

"This is why I love Cornwall," the Major said breaking the silence. He turned to look at Elizabeth.

"We've been a pair of old duffers," she said. "I knew I should not have doubted you."

"Me likewise," he smiled. "Now I hope you will let me take you to that dinner we spoke about last time."

"Of course," she beamed. Her eyes were smiling again, and he slid his arm out of sling, took her in his arms and gently kissed her forehead. She raised her face and they kissed for a long time.

"Penny for them," said the sergeant as he put an enamel mug of tea and a sandwich on a plate down on the table in front of Elizabeth. She looked up at him and apologised, having been unaware she was so engrossed in her thoughts. It was lunchtime and Elizabeth was sat in a small Nissen hut amongst the trees behind St Catherine's Fort which had guarded the harbour entrance to Fowey since the days of Henry VIII. Training posters covered the walls with everything from aircraft recognition silhouettes to slogans reminding troops to keep their rifles clean. The Major was inspecting the guns and defences at the southernmost point of the Bodmin Stop Line. He had requested his driver be given some sustenance while he made his tour of the latest additions to this old fort which carried evidence of each time Britain had been under threat of invasion since the 1540s. Elizabeth had sat in the small mess hut and lost herself in thoughts of that kiss on the road overlooking Lostwithiel. He was so gentle, so tender. She had felt a strange warmth course through her veins as she felt his lips pressing hers. Was she falling in love? Was that possible? It was only nine months since the news of the dreadful loss of her fiancé's ship? She remembered him in his sailor's uniform asking her father for her hand in marriage on his last leave in August 1939. He, although only in his mid-twenties, was a stickler for 'doing things proper', as he used to say. But Elizabeth had never experienced a sensation like that educed by the passionate embrace of the Major. Her fiancé's kisses had been awkward, almost mechanical, without the natural intensity of today's. She had felt drawn to the Major since he first walked in at the end of the service on Sunday, but this was stupid. She hardly knew him. He was a bit older than her. Then so was her fiancé, but the Major was a few more years on that too. Twenty-eight was her guess, but she'd have to subtly discover the actual figure. She had just turned twenty-one. She would have to ask him on the way back to Bodmin. She would enjoy getting to know the Major.

Elizabeth decided she could not share all this with the sergeant so she thanked him and he left her to return to the cook who was bemoaning that the milk from the farm was late. She bowed her head in a silent prayer of gratitude for the good things she was enjoying that day and then tucked in heartily to the sandwich. If this was love, it certainly gave her an appetite.

It was just gone two o'clock when a soldier stuck his head round the door to say the Major was ready to leave. He was stood out on the small parade ground. They exited the North Gate and walked down the rocky path to the road at Readymoney beach where she had left the car. Across the beach soldiers were erecting scaffolding that would prevent craft landing at the beach, especially if they were to set off one of the mines that would eventually be attached to it. Others were constructing a sandbag gun position on top of what in its day had been a limekiln but now looked more like a castle folly. Elizabeth took the rotor arm out of her breast pocket and lifted the bonnet to replace it. Leaving a car without immobilising it was now an offence, and she had obeyed what the driver's instruction course at the Depot had shown her.

The car started at the first time of asking. As she pulled away up the hill and drove past Neptune Point, she glanced across at the Major.

"Where now, sir?" she asked.

"Please, when we are alone, do drop the formality," he replied before answering her question. "We need to look at some defences on the other side of the river, so we'll have to take the ferry. It's up the other end of town in Passage Street, so just keep going until we get to it."

"Thank you, sir," she replied emphasising the last word to show she had fully understood his request. She couldn't keep a straight face and ended up chuckling out loud. He shook his head in mock bemusement.

Elizabeth had to slow to walking pace as she negotiated the corners and pedestrians in South Street by the parish church. Fore Street was not much better and it wasn't until they had negotiated Custom House Hill and were through the narrows by the chapel in North Street that she could change up a gear. The road soon became Passage Street and then there was the steep slipway down to the ferry. There was a small van in the queue and Elizabeth pulled up behind it.

In a minute or two the ferry arrived. It was a floating raft attached to a small motor boat that powered the three or four vehicles across at a time. An army motorbike and sidecar combination came off the ferry and then Elizabeth followed the van down to the water's edge and up the ramp onto the ferry. She had never driven onto a ferry before, but she tried hard not to let her nerves show. She was grateful there was a van in front as she feared she would not stop in the right place and drop off the front of the raft. There were no gates or barriers, just a ferryman in boots and a sailor's cap directing affairs.

"Put your parking brake on and turn off your engine, please miss," the wizened faced ferryman instructed. "No charge if you are on army business."

The Major, impressed at the generosity of spirit, expressed his thanks.

"I shall more than double my prices if Jerry ever gets here," said the ferryman with a grin.

"We shall do our best to see that he doesn't," replied the Major. "Can't have you profiteering from the war, now, can we?"

"Been enough of a struggle to stay afloat this last ten year," the old man said before turning his attention to the van in front.

Soon the ferry was chugging across the narrow stretch of river, the old ferryman helping to steer the raft by means of a giant oar attached to one side. The ferry had plied its trade at this point since the fourteenth century, and Elizabeth wondered just how many years of service the old ferryman had seen. As they approached the landing slip at Bodinnick, she could see a large white sign that had been painted over so as to deny any local knowledge to the enemy should he arrive. She laughed as the lettering that said 'The Old Ferry Inn' was clearly visible through the freshly applied paint.

"It'll need a few more coats before you can't read that," she said pointing it out to the Major. He nodded but his eyes were scanning either side of the slip looking for any sign of defences that would prevent the invader getting ashore. There were none. The ferry announced its arrival with a slight bump as the ramp rode up the slipway. Elizabeth started the engine, engaged first gear and gently drove off, grateful to be safely on terra firma once more. They squeezed through the gap between the wall and the ferry office. The van turned left but the Major indicated he wanted to go straight on up the hill. About 50 yards up the hill he asked Elizabeth to stop. There on the right hand side a small detachment of soldiers was busy building a pillbox. The Major got out, looked back down the hill at the ferry slipway, and having satisfied himself that the field of fire would prevent a successful landing, turned to speak to the troops. Elizabeth watched. The Major certainly had rank and an air of authority, but he didn't lord it over the other ranks. He seemed capable of winning one's respect by his speech and the sense you soon gained that he was genuinely interested in what you were doing. He never demeaned his rank, his position or his social standing but he connected with people. He was a genuine leader. He led by example, with integrity. In no time the soldiers were smiling as the Major squeezed his way into the midst of the half constructed Type 24 pillbox. But as he came to leave a couple of minutes later they stood to attention and saluted as one man. They had fallen for his charms as well, Elizabeth mused. "If hardened soldiers succumb after just a few minutes, what hope have I?" she asked herself as she watched him walk past the bonnet and round to the passenger door.

"Another fifty yards or so up the hill please, driver" he said emphasising the last word in a way that mimicked her earlier remark. Elizabeth sensed the connecting of a shared sense of humour.

"I'm looking for the entrance to a pathway off to the right," the Major said. "The soldiers said it was by the school and the well."

"That must be it," said Elizabeth bringing the car to a halt on the steep hill where a path made its way between two buildings and disappeared under the trees behind.

"I'll only be five minutes," said the Major. "You'd best stay with the car." With that he was gone leaving Elizabeth wondering just how long she would be able to enjoy his company. She had already lost the man to whom she had been engaged, she didn't want this war to take another. She shuddered. She must put all thought of death out of her mind. But then, this war could take the Major away alive and she might not see him for a long time. After all, wasn't he here on some secret business from London? He would be returning there some time soon. What was she to do then? The war wouldn't last for ever she told herself. But what if the Germans did come? The emotions washed over her and then ebbed again as she rationalised the situation. Would she ever know true romance and be able to marry and know the intimacy of a husband's love? Oh how she wished. She sighed. Our times are in God's hands. Only He can save our nation now. But in a strange way, she thought she ought to be grateful for this war for it had brought the Major into her life and she had never felt such happiness as the two occasions he had taken her into his arms and kissed her. There was only one thing for it. She would enjoy each and every moment. She'd had her time for mourning. Now wasn't this the time to dance? She would savour it and not worry how long it all might last. Do not worry about tomorrow for tomorrow will worry about itself.

Within ten minutes the Major had returned from inspecting another pillbox being constructed above the natural harbour of the river estuary. He said there was another he needed to check on and gave instructions through the lanes past the tidal creek of Pont Pill and up onto the hill at the back of Polruan. They stopped by a roadblock. The Major spoke briefly with the soldiers on duty. They indicated the car should be backed into a track off the road. Again Elizabeth was asked to wait in the car while the Major disappeared down the track across the fields towards the river. Elizabeth enjoyed the sense that what she was contributing to was important. Quite how, she didn't know, but she was drawn to the air of mystery that surrounded the Major. The soldiers stood awkwardly not knowing whether they should engage the pretty driver in conversation. They were obviously discussing her, the car and what on earth the Major was doing as they kept looking her way. Elizabeth was glad when a horse and cart came along the lane and gave them something to do.

Eventually the Major returned and informed her they could now return to Bodmin. He had seen enough for the day to be able to report back to London. He suggested, if she was off duty later, he be allowed to take her to dinner this evening.

"That would be lovely," she responded. "There's a concert being put on in town as well. We could always take that in afterwards if you are agreeable." He was and the rest of the drive back to the Depot passed in thoughts of what dress she would wear. She had only brought two from home and couldn't make up her mind which would suit the occasion better. She may not have her Major for long but she was going to enjoy every minute of it.

Chapter 17

It was six o'clock as the Major stood by the War Memorial waiting for Elizabeth to arrive. The bronze trooper stood on his granite plinth with the names of those from the Duke of Cornwall's Light Infantry who had made the ultimate sacrifice in the Great War carved below. The Major wondered what would become of him in this war. Was he being fair in letting Elizabeth get close to him? He was due to return to London tomorrow. His week was up. Churchill wanted his report in person. How could he tell her without spoiling her evening? Should he indicate that this evening would be the finale in their dalliance? That would be the honourable thing to do, but the more he pondered on it the less he liked the idea. He had been strangely drawn to this young woman since the moment he had set eyes on her. Her beauty was beguiling. Her company was enlivening. She obviously had feelings for him as the icy reception this morning had shown until she realised that he had not flirted with Kara Johns the evening he dropped her off drunk at her parent's house. Elizabeth kissed him with a passion he had never experienced before. It awoke in him a longing, a yearning for her that went to the very core of his being. He would be back in Cornwall again he was sure. Besides he would visit his parents when he had leave, though that might now have to wait if he was to visit Elizabeth. He would take her to see them. I must be serious he thought. But he knew his parents would be bowled over by Elizabeth's charms. I would be a fool if I let such a beauty go.

A steam whistle penetrated his train of thought and he turned towards the railway where a train was departing the station. A young woman with blonde hair dressed in a blue summer dress and a white cardigan was walking towards him from the Lostwithiel road. Her long hair, gathered through a slide, was hanging down her back. Her blue eyes were sparkling. The slender lines of her face radiated a natural beauty that did not need to be enhanced by make-up. The Major couldn't detect any trace of it and thought a Hollywood star could learn a thing or two. Her long legs strode with a purpose. He was mesmerised. He would not be letting this beauty go until his dying day.

"Do I look okay for a Major to take to dinner?" she asked doing a swirl that made her dress billow and her hair swish in a fan behind her.

"You look fit for the Ritz," the Major replied. "How did you manage it in such a short time? Not that you don't look lovely normally," he added quickly, "but I will have every soldier in town staring in jealousy at the beautiful woman on my arm."

"You've dispensed with the sling," Elizabeth remarked noticing it was missing for the first time.

"More nuisance than help now," he replied offering his good arm. They set off down the street past the station into town arm in arm. The Major began whistling the melody "I'm stepping out with a memory tonight."

"So who thinks you are crazy to be stepping out with me?" said Elizabeth using the lyrics to tease him.

"Nobody. I just want this evening to be special," he said interrupting the tune.

"Well cocktails for two will be nice," said Elizabeth smiling, "to say nothing of a kiss in a taxi, though I'm not sure the parks round here are big enough to have hansom cabs."

"After dark you may not need a hansom!" the Major retorted.

"I'm not too sure which way to take that," said Elizabeth laughing. Both of them were deeply engaged in conversation as they made their way down St Nicholas Street. They did not notice a melancholy young woman stood at an attic window watching them as they passed wondering where on earth her young love was and what had happened to him.

The dining room at the Royal Hotel was nearly full when the Major and Elizabeth arrived. However, the thoughtful Major had telephoned to reserve a table and they were shown to a quiet table in a small alcove on one side of the room. Once the waiter had taken their order, Elizabeth relaxed and smiled across the table.

"I want to know all there is to know about you," she said.

"Then you'll be in for a dull evening. There's not a lot to tell," replied the Major.

"Oh, don't do yourself an injustice," cautioned Elizabeth. "They don't make any Tom, Dick or Harry a Major in the British army, so there must be something to you."

"Happy childhood, school, university and then the army. That's about it."

"Come on, there must be more than that!" exclaimed Elizabeth realising that getting any information about someone who worked in Intelligence was going to be hard work. "What made your childhood happy?"

The Major thought for a moment and then said, "Love. My brother and I were loved. It meant that we never had to worry about a thing. Sure there were sad times and life's ups and downs but in them all we knew we were loved. The older I get the more I realise I have a lot to be grateful for to my parents."

"Did you get on with your brother or did you fight like all brothers do?"

"We had our moments but we enjoyed each other's company. My brother is three years older than me, so I felt it when he went up to Oxford to read languages."

"Is that where you studied?" enquired Elizabeth thinking how handsome his face was when he smiled.

"No. I was at King's College, London. I studied under Major General Maurice who was the Professor of Military Studies there."

"Did you enjoy life in London?" asked Elizabeth who had never ventured much further than Plymouth.

"As a student you have a partial view of a city like London. I enjoyed my studies and my time there, but the hustle and bustle, the dirt and the grime did make me glad to come down to Cornwall at term's end."

"So you were set on a career in the Army from quite young?"

"I guess I was impressed by the marching bands that came into town when I was a young boy during the Great War. Once I was older I thought it was an opportunity to travel, to see the Empire, and to get some experience of the world before settling back in England, but this war has put paid to all that. We are now fighting for more than just the opportunity to live your dreams."

"But that's just it. Live your dreams, and not what some Hitler says you should be. Free to be who you are and think what you think. You know, I think Hitler would have to put most of England in one of his work camps if he ever conquered us."

"Well, let's hope we never have to find out."

"So what does your brother do?"

"He's the intelligent one. He got a first in languages. He then got a job working for the American press in Vienna. He moved out there in '35, met and married a local lass in '36 and they had a son within the year." The Major's tone had become serious.

"Impressive. Where are your brother and his family now?" asked Elizabeth sensing the concern.

"I wish I knew," said the Major honestly.

"You told me at the farm you haven't heard from them for a while," said Elizabeth gently.

"The last letter I received was in February 1939. That was the last anyone in the family has heard."

"I'm sorry," said Elizabeth putting out a hand to touch his. He seemed grateful at the show of sympathy, but it was short-lived as the waiter arrived with their meals and the moment passed and the conversation moved on.

The audience were applauding loudly as the couple slipped in at the back of the concert at the Public Rooms. The hall was full for the first concert that had been put together by the YMCA's entertainments man Len White. Some of Elizabeth's ATS colleagues had been roped into forming a concert party with some of the soldiers, which is why she was keen to put in an appearance in the audience. Elizabeth, thanks to the timing of her weekend home, had managed to resist Sergeant Buscombe's recruitment drive.

"Now for a little dance number," the compere was announcing as they found two seats on the end of a row near the back. The troops in the audience whistled loudly as a group of female dancers high kicked their way onto the stage and rotated round several times like a can-can line.

"Your lot, I assume," asked the Major above the din.

"Yes, the one on the left is Molly. She's in the bunk next to me back in the dorm." laughed Elizabeth. "What a hoot!"

The group of chiffon-clad girls then parted to reveal a young Jamaican tap dancer who took centre stage.

"He's good," whispered the Major who, although he was no authority on any kind of dance, was impressed with the fellow's fancy footwork.

"That's Stanley Coleman," replied Elizabeth. "The girls all like him. Molly says he learnt to dance at the Fred Astaire School in America."

The dancers finished their routine to tremendous applause. With Stanley Coleman in the middle they took a bow.

"Let's hear it for the Bombshells," shouted the compere returning to the stage as the dancers exited to the sides and the whistles rang out again.

The concert continued for another hour. It was a mix of songs and solos, a sketch which poked fun at barrack life, several more dance routines from the Bombshells and all expertly accompanied by Burt Brewes, the pianist, who had been an arranger at Chappells, the music publishers in London, before getting his call up papers. Finally all the performers returned to the stage with the compere and took their bow before a delighted audience who then stood and joined in a rousing rendition of 'God Save The King'.

"Are you coming down to the canteen for a drink?" asked a couple of young women in ATS uniform who had spotted Elizabeth in the crowd as they made their way out. The YMCA ran a canteen for the services in the rooms below the hall with an entrance on Mount Folly. Elizabeth glanced at the Major for direction.

"Thank you for your kind invitation but Elizabeth and I thought we'd take advantage of the final hour of daylight by taking a stroll up to the Beacon," replied the Major puzzled at the fit of giggles his reply caused. Elizabeth's two colleagues disappeared into the crowd singing "Don't go walking down lover's lane with anyone else but me". Elizabeth took the Major's arm thinking she was in for some ribbing when she got back to her dormitory in the barracks but she was happy at the prospect of having the Major to herself for the next hour.

The couple exited the Public Rooms and walked up the hill by the Head Post Office. It was steep so the pace was slow but they were just thrilled to be enjoying each other's company. As they reached the lane at the top they stopped and looked back at the hill they had climbed. The parish church looked like a model nestled in the town below.

"That's some hill," said Elizabeth her cheeks glowing with the exertion.

"Let's go up to the monument and we can sit on it and have a rest," replied the Major.

They crossed the lane and continued up the grass track towards the open expanse of the common land that had long been the favourite haunt of local lovers and promenaders. The Cornwall militia had trained here one hundred years before and it was the chosen site for the national monument to Sir Walter Raleigh Gilbert. The couple made their way to the towering obelisk and, climbing on the vast granite blocks, they sat down absorbing the view northwards that took in the downs above Wadebridge right up to the tors of Bodmin Moor. They said nothing as they took in the beauty of their surroundings.

It was the Major who first broke the silence. "I am blessed to be in such a beautiful place with such a beautiful woman."

Elizabeth smiled and leaned in towards him. He kissed her on the lips, gently at first and then more passionately. She put her arms round his waist and pulled him in closer. He put one hand in under her hair and gently stroked the nape of her neck.

She closed her eyes and wallowed in the sensation that his tingling touch was bringing to her body. He ran his fingers up and down her spine as their breathing became faster.

Suddenly he pulled away. "Sorry," he panted. "Someone's coming." In the distance a figure in a long coat and carrying a duffel bag was walking towards the monument. The couple sat with arms around each other and watched him as he got closer. The man acknowledged them and walked past the monument before disappearing through a small gateway in the hedge. He was a member of the Observer Corps reporting to his post for duty.

Once the man was gone the Major spoke. "Elizabeth, I have to go back to London tomorrow." He paused as she groaned. "But I want to ask whether you would be my girl. I will write and every leave I get I will do my best to come and see you. That's if you'll agree to have me as the man you walk out with."

"You have to leave so soon," she said more as a statement than a question. "But I will be right here waiting for you when you return to Cornwall." She looked into his eyes and felt the love they expressed for her.

"You had better write to me every week at least or you'll be in trouble," she teased.

"Every letter I send will include one of these," he said pulling her close and kissing her again. His fingers danced up her spine and then in gentle strokes brushed down her shoulder blades and down her back, only to go round once again, and again. The sun was dipping down behind Mulberry Pit and the monument cast a long thin shadow. The shrill ringing song of a mistle thrush perched high on a nearby hedgerow before it nestled down for the night provided a dreamy accompaniment to the young sweethearts.

Elizabeth shivered. The air was turning colder now the warmth of the sun was fast fading. The Major stood up on the giant step below them. He undid his jacket and swung it round onto Elizabeth's shoulders.

"Now you'll get cold," she said.

"Not with you to cuddle into," he said and wormed his hands in under the jacket and round her waist. "One last kiss."

"I've never met anyone like you," Elizabeth said honestly. "You can be the comic book hero soldier leaping onto trains, but you are also a warm and romantic gentleman. Thank you for a lovely evening."

"Does your God ever give people second chances?" asked the Major.

"What do you mean 'my God'?" Elizabeth responded wondering what on earth had provoked such a question from the handsome young officer in her arms. "If there is a God, and I firmly believe there is, then he is everyone's God or he is not God at all but just a figment of our imaginations."

"Yes, yes, I know that," said the Major. "That's not what I meant. You seem to know God. The Almighty seems real to you and your family, not just some distant Providence and I thought you might have some experience that would help answer my question."

"The Old Testament is full of people who messed up or thought life had passed them by and then God gave them a second chance. Abraham thought he was too old for a son. Joseph must have wondered if his dreams would ever come true as he spent time in an Egyptian prison. Moses even killed a man before leading the people out of Egypt. Rahab was a harlot but was saved when Jericho fell. Ruth was a widow in a foreign country but then found her true love. King David had an affair and then had the husband murdered but went on to write some of the greatest poetry about repentance. Elijah was definitely suicidal at one point. Jonah ran away from God; well, at least he tried. But both prophets were given the chance to continue their mission."

"But today, do you think God still does it today?" interrupted the Major.

"My father said Dunkirk was a miracle that has given the country a second chance. The reports said that Hitler's tanks stopped when they could have rolled our army completely into the sea, and then when the little boats set out the sea became calm. If that isn't God giving us a second chance…"

"I can see what you are saying," the Major cut in again. "But I want to know if God gives second chances to people like us, you and me, today.'

Elizabeth looked at him: the man of her dreams, the one who had stirred her heart, her passions, her intellect, her soul. Less than a week ago she had wallowed in misery wondering if she would ever find love again, her affections wrecked in the icy waters of Scapa Flow. You just never know what a day is going to bring forth.

"Yes I do," she said, the belief resonating in her voice. "You are my evidence."

"But if you didn't do something you should have, will God give you a second chance to make amends?" the Major asked. There was an earnestness in his questioning that made Elizabeth realise he was beginning to trust her with a burden that he carried close to his heart.

"While you have breath you can always seek to put things right," she said.

"Thank you." The words were barely audible as he kissed her gently on the lips.

"Major! Major!" The cry was anguished and breathless. The couple looked up to see Captain Cregoe running towards them. They climbed down off the monument as he covered the final twenty yards.

"He's broken cover, sir," said the red faced Captain. "He tried to force his way through a road block out near the Wireless Station. They are scouring the downs for him now, sir."

"Have you got a car?" the Major asked.

"Yes sir, it's down by the road. I couldn't get it through the blocks to get it right up here."

"Right let's go," he said to the Captain. Then turning to Elizabeth he added, "I think you'd better come too. I can't leave you here."

The three set off running across the Beacon towards the car.

"You are a hard man to find, Major!" puffed the Captain.

"Can't a man enjoy a walk when he's off duty?" retorted the Major with a smile.

"The gatehouse told us you'd left the Barracks, so I've been searching all over town. Finally some ATS girls in the YMCA canteen told me where I'd most likely find you though I shan't repeat exactly what they said."

"I can imagine," laughed Elizabeth. "Just wait until I catch up with them!"

The Captain had brought the Major's car. It was parked beyond a set of granite blocks which had been put across the narrow entrance that led up to the Beacon above the Board School to prevent the easy movement of enemy vehicles should they invade this part of Cornwall. He held open the door for Elizabeth to get in the back while the Major slid in the front. The Captain started the engine and pulled away with such fury he left a cloud of dust behind them. He headed down the lane, past the Land Army Hostel and down the hill to the White Clock Tower. The Tower was a memorial to the five staff from St Lawrence's Mental Hospital who died in the Great War. Here he had to stop and declare his business at the chicane and road block but was quickly allowed through. He accelerated down the A30 past the half built Catholic Church where they had abandoned work for the duration and through an avenue of trees that took them past the entrance to St Lawrence's Mental Hospital, as the Cornwall Asylum was now known.

"So fill me in on what's happened," the Major said turning to the Captain feeling he would be able to answer now they were on a straight piece of road.

"We got a radio call to the Barracks from the Wireless Station saying a car coming from the west had driven through the first road block, had failed to get through the second road block but had made off across the downs on the cart tracks. The soldiers at the second block are certain they hit the car as it veered off the main road. They don't think it will get too far; one of them seemed to think he hit the radiator."

"Where do the cart tracks he's gone down lead?" enquired the Major.

"I don't know. They just said there were lots of farm tracks that criss-crossed the downs."

"How do you know it's our man?"

"The soldiers on the first road block got a good look at him and were able to describe him well. I'm pretty certain it's our man."

"But he's got away? He could be anywhere by now. Do we need to call out more men?"

"They have called out their other section and begun to scour the downs before it gets too dark to see."

"How many men have they got posted out there?"

"They would have eight on duty on the two roadblocks, another eight off duty in the hut they've got up there at Redtye, and goodness knows where the third section in the platoon would be. I guess the wireless station is pretty important to guard from the Jerry."

"Yes, it was set up by Marconi but is now under Cable & Wireless. It transmits all Britain's wireless messages to Canada and South Africa."

As the Captain drove into the centre of the village of Lanivet he was greeted by the sight of two farmers with pitchforks standing in front of a hand cart and bales of hay that formed a makeshift road block from the Village Inn across to the Wesleyan Chapel.

"Did you call out the LDV?" asked the Major.

"No, but we'll soon find out if this is connected," replied the Captain. He slowed the car and wound down the window. He could see that both men were wearing LDV arm bands.

"Sorry to stop ee," the younger of the two men said. "Us been told to check vehicles coming through village."

"Why's that?" asked the Captain.

"Well as you'm army I s'pose I can tell ee. Some of our men heard shooting comin' from up Innis where the Wireless Station be. Cap'n May has taken a patrol up there to see what's what."

"That's where we're heading," said the Captain, "if you'd be kind enough to let us through."

"O'course, though it's been quiet up there for 'bout an hour now."

"Just keep a look out for the suspect. He's a young blond haired man, in his twenties, speaks with a bit of an accent and may pass himself off as Dutch. Just be careful he's probably armed," said the Major leaning across to speak to the LDV man. Seeing the worried expression on the farmer's face and the pitchfork he grasped in his right hand the Captain added, "If you see him just phone in a report."

"How's we gonna do that?" the LDV man asked. "Nearest phone is at the white house at the bottom of Westheath in Bodmin."

"It's alright Talwynn," said the older man speaking for the first time. "Cap'n May has recruited one of the Thomas boys on his bicycle to act as messenger. We'll get word to you, sir. Now Talwynn let's shift this cart so we don't delay these officers anymore."

The farmers thrust their pitchforks into a bale of hay with a ferocity that made Elizabeth wince. "They would do a German mischief with those if they got close enough," she said. The LDV men released the brake, each took a shaft and rolled the cart to one side to allow the Captain to drive through the chicane created by the hay bales.

"I'm not so sure how effective that would be against a German tank," said the Major as the Captain accelerated away.

"At least it shows a spirit of defiance," said the Captain, "and anything that slows Jerry down will be helpful for the regular troops."

The road wound its way through a wooded valley before climbing and emerging on Innis Downs. On the left a line of modern villas stood proudly. They had been built for the workers at the Wireless Station. Very soon the Captain brought the car to a halt at the roadblock where a soldier covered their approach with his rifle while the other raised his arm indicating they should stop. Both the Major and the Captain jumped out to talk to the men who called for their Corporal to address the officers.

155

"We've found the car, sir. It was abandoned about a mile south of here by a Bible Christian chapel. A bullet through the radiator meant it had soon overheated and so he's taken off on foot."

"Do you know which way he's headed?" asked the Major.

"If he keeps to the paths or tracks he will end up either at Criggan or Lockengate. We have sent men down both routes in the hope of catching up with him and Williams has taken the motorcycle to go round and look along the road to Bugle which is where both routes will come out if he continues heading south."

"Can we see the car?" asked the Captain. Turning to the Major he added, "It may contain some clues on his movements."

"Jump in the front," said the Major to the Corporal. "You can direct us. I'm sure your men can spare you for ten minutes."

The Major climbed in the back next to Elizabeth. The Corporal indicated they should drive towards the Wireless Station. As they got closer to the huge lattice masts that towered in a line he told the corporal to look for a track off to the left. The Captain slowed as the Corporal pointed. It was a sharp turn heading back across the Downs. The Captain had to reverse as he couldn't swing round in one go. The car bounced along the track. They came to a couple of junctions where the rough tracks criss-crossed the Downs. The Corporal instructed them to keep going straight on.

Eventually they came to a small chapel in a burial ground. The chapel had been built in 1820 on land that had been a Quaker burial ground by William O'Bryan, the founder of the Bible Christian Connection. It was a small austere building with two windows on the side. At an angle to the hedge was a black Ford Eight with its bonnet left up. There was a bullet hole in the rear window and another just above the bumper. The soldiers on the roadblock had obviously found their target as it had driven away from them. Four LDV men scrambled to their feet as the car approached.

Pulling up by the Ford, the four of them got out and looked at the damage. The Captain opened the passenger's door and looked in. A .303 bullet was embedded in the dashboard, presumably the shot that had penetrated the rear window. 'Just a matter of inches,' he thought, 'from nailing their quarry.' Otherwise the car was empty. The Captain checked under the seats and in the glove box for any clues but their man had left none. The old policeman acknowledged the work of a professional.

"Apart from getting some fingerprints, I don't think this is going to help us much," said the Captain backing out of the car to address the Major.

"So which are the ways he could have gone?" the Major asked the Corporal.

"The track goes down across the fields to Crift and Innisvath, but there's also a footpath that goes along by the old sand pits below Trescoll and comes out at Lockengate. We've sent men down each of them."

"But no reports back?"

"No sir. Not yet."

"I think we are done here. We will get the police out to deal with the car. We'll give you a lift back to the road block." Turning to the LDV men he said, "Make sure no one touches the car until the police get here."

The four clambered aboard the Humber Snipe and the Captain had to do a several point turn to get the car turned round in the lane. The sky was purple as the last vestiges of light were all that remained of the day. The masts of the wireless station pointed heavenwards like dark fingers. The Captain wondered what else they could achieve until the morrow. He drove slowly back to the A30 and stopped at the roadblock.

Just as the Major was thanking the Corporal for his assistance, a motorcycle with its headlight dimmed by the mask was bouncing along the track that came from Castle Hill. He pulled onto the A30 and rolled up to the road block. A soldier was riding the BSA M20. All three soldiers in the Snipe got out. The motorcyclist drew up and said excitedly,

"He's caught the train. He made it to Bugle on foot. The station master there said he ran and caught the train."

"In which direction?" asked the Major.

"St Blazey. Apparently it was the last train down for the evening," replied the young soldier on the bike. Williams could not have been more than nineteen but was clearly enjoying the excitement providing him with the opportunity to race around the Cornish countryside on a powerful machine.

"How long ago did the train leave Bugle?" The Major's tone was urgent.

"It left," the young soldier paused as he looked at his wrist watch, "just fifteen minutes ago. I could only have missed it by a minute or two. I came straight back."

The Major turned to the Corporal. "Get on the radio. Get some men down to St Blazey and Par stations as quick as possible. Anyone. The troops from the coastal battery there, the LDV or even the local bobby. Once he gets there we could lose him again as he could go towards Penzance or Plymouth or Fowey. If he left fifteen minutes ago he'll be arriving any time in the next five minutes and if he's got to wait a few minutes for a connection we may catch him up. Jump to it."

"Yes sir," The Corporal climbed on the back of the motorcycle and ordered the soldier to head for the wireless station.

"I assume we are going there as well," said the Captain as the officers turned back towards the Snipe. Elizabeth was sat in the back watching wondering just what the excitement was. Walking out with the Major was certainly interesting. The concert seemed a long time ago although only a couple of hours had passed since they walked up Crinnick's Hill to the Beacon. The two men got in and the car sped off into the gathering gloom.

Chapter 18

The Major stood on the curved platform of Fowey Station looking at the quiet and empty scene around him. Behind him was the station building with its collection of offices and waiting rooms. Above him the station canopy stood silhouetted against a clear dark sky, a strong moon providing the light. He walked to the end of the platform and looked down on the river. The ferry that plied its traffic across to Bodinnick lay at its mooring. He walked back to the waiting Captain and Elizabeth.

"Who was on platform duty when that last train came in?" he asked more of himself than expecting a reply from his companions. "Let's find the Station Master," he added as they turned back towards the station entrance. They made their way to the large, imposing station master's house. Its slate roof shone in the moonlight. The Major knocked loudly and soon the station master could be heard drawing back the bolt on the door. He stepped out in his shirt sleeves, having removed his tie and jacket on finishing his duties for the day.

"Good evening gentlemen, miss," he said somewhat surprised at the callers. "What can I do for you at this hour? I hope it's not a train you're wanting as there are none until six-thirty in the morning."

The Major explained their enquiry, described for whom they were looking, and paused waiting for a response.

"The last train is always busy these days. You know sailors and soldiers, returning from a night out, not always in uniform. I was on the platform with Wendon who was collecting the tickets. There were several blonde haired young men who passed through, but it's rare that any of them speak. They just hold out their ticket. One or two may mutter a 'Thank you' or a 'Good night' but nothing I recall that would make me think any of them was a foreigner. I'm sorry I can't rule out that he did pass through, but I cannot say he definitely did either. I can phone Wendon if you like."

The Major nodded, and as they were shown inside muttered something to the Captain about not leaving any stone unturned. The Station Master waited until they had all stepped inside, drew the black-out curtain across the door and then switched on the electric light. In a couple of minutes he had phoned his employee, let the

Major describe the person he was looking for, but all to no avail. Wendon said pretty much the same as the station master. Several fitting the description had passed through but nothing to make any stand out as being suspicious or foreign. The Major apologised for the intrusion and thanked the station master for his co-operation, and then led the Captain and Elizabeth back to the car.

"Back to Bodmin," said the Major once all three were inside.

"Giving up for the night," asked the Captain as he started the car.

"Not for a minute," smiled the Major. "We're going to talk to the one person I believe will know where our man is heading."

The Captain looked across at the Major, opened his mouth to say something, but thought better of it. He engaged the gear and the car pulled away up Passage Lane and past the Mortuary.

"Will you drop me back to the Barracks?" asked Elizabeth. "If I'm late past midnight I shall get a rollicking from Sergeant Buscombe."

The Captain glanced at his watch in the moonlight. It was a quarter to one. 'Too late to avoid that one,' he thought but said nothing.

"I was rather hoping you would accompany us to this meeting. We might appreciate a woman's presence," the Major replied.

"I'll willingly come, just as long as you sort it with Sergeant Buscombe in the morning." said Elizabeth.

"One of the advantages of rank," smiled the Major. "Especially if I tell her how you were helping an important matter of national security."

The Captain looked even more intrigued as to what part Elizabeth might play in the search for their man, but drove in silence, taking the Bodmin road at Four Turnings.

Half an hour later the Captain quietly eased the car to a stop outside the house in St Nicholas Street. It was only when they entered Bodmin up the hill by the Dragon Pits, the town rubbish dump, that the Major enlightened his companions as to who they were going to visit. The Captain had been hoping the Major would call it a night. After all, it had been quite an evening rushing hither and thither but alas with nothing to show for it. The old policeman in him would have called time and reassessed the situation and their resources in the cold light of another day. But the Major had a determination about him that the Captain could only admire.

The three of them got out of the car and looked at the house in darkness. 'Was it really only a week ago that he had first called here with the Major?' The Captain shook his head in disbelief at all that had passed since he had first accepted the Major's offer of a lift back from Lostwithiel.

With a sense of deja-vu, the Captain opened the wooden porch door and knocked on the inside door. It took three loud knocks before there was sound of movement inside the house. Mrs Johns gingerly opened the door just a fraction and peered round. Her hair was in curlers. She wore a striped dressing gown hitched at the waist with a cord.

"What on earth…," she started saying sounding annoyed, but then she recognised the Captain and the Major. "Oh, it's you. I don't know what you can be wanting at this ungodly hour, but you better come in." She showed them into the front room.

"Do sit down, please," Mrs Johns sounded flustered. The Major remained standing.

"It's your daughter we have come to see," said the Major matter of factly.

"What on earth has she done now?" Memories of Wednesday's delivery of her drunken daughter were still fresh in her mind.

"I think she may have some vital information. Is she here?" The tone of the Major's voice indicated he was in no mood for any lack of co-operation. Mrs Johns nodded. "Then," the Major continued, "Could you kindly bring her down so we can speak. I am afraid it cannot wait until morning."

Mrs Johns scurried out of the room and the sound of her footsteps disappeared up the stairs. A couple of minutes later she ushered her daughter into the front room. The young woman, who had obviously been woken from her sleep, was dressed in a silk dressing gown, tied tightly at the waist accentuating the hour glass figure. As she sat she ran a hand through her wavy hair in an attempt to tame it. She waited for the officers to speak.

"I'm sorry to have to wake you at this hour," the Major began, "But I have reason to believe you weren't quite honest with us last time we spoke."

"I had drunk a little too much, and if I said anything I shouldn't, then I apologise, but that's hardly a reason for dragging a young woman out of her bed in the middle of the night, especially when I've got to be at work early in the morning."

The Major realised his mistake and rephrased his question. "I was not referring to that occasion, Miss Johns, but the last time the Captain and I spoke with you here about the young Dutchman who had been staying here."

"I answered all your questions then. I've got nothing else to add," said Kara defiantly looking at her three visitors in turn.

"I'm sure she has, sir," her mother added. "My Harry gave her a long talking to after you left on Tuesday."

"You told us that you went for a drive with him one evening. We would like to ask you a bit more about that occasion," said the Major.

From the look on Mrs John's face it was obvious this was the first she had heard of this. She stared intently at her daughter, wishing her husband was here to help in yet another situation in which she was rapidly feeling out of her depth.

Kara said nothing. She merely crossed her legs and pulled the dressing gown in around them.

"You said that you went for a drive after dark and headed out of Bodmin towards Respryn." The Major was stood in front of the fireplace, his hands clasped together behind his back.

"I did."

"Where did you go?"

"I told you I don't know. We went down one lane after another. Respryn was the only place I recognised. I've walked out to the bridge there before. Once we were beyond that I didn't have a clue."

"You didn't see anywhere else you recognised?"

"One lane looks like another in the dark."

"You didn't catch the name of a house or a shop?"

"It was all country lanes. We didn't go through any towns. I can tell you for certain I did not see any shops."

"Or pubs?" the Captain spoke for the first time.

"Or pubs," repeated Kara.

"How long were you travelling?" asked the Major. Kara paused before answering. The Major was happy to give her thinking time.

"At least half an hour I'd say. Could be up to an hour. I don't have a watch so it is a bit hard to be exact," said Kara with a shrug of the shoulders.

"Where did you go?" the Major repeated the question.

"I've told you I don't know."

"You said that when you got there Johann left you in the car?" The Major paused, looking at the young woman for confirmation. She nodded.

"You said he was gone for about half an hour. Where did he go?"

"I don't know. It was dark. I couldn't see."

"What did he do?"

"I don't know."

"Did he meet someone?"

"Not that I saw."

"Did you see anyone else at all?"

"No."

"Did you hear anything?"

"No."

"What did he do?"

"I don't know." Kara's voice was sounding tired at the repetition of the questions.

"Did he take anything with him?"

"He took something out of the boot but I didn't see what."

"You didn't get a glimpse of it at all?"

"No."

"You said he was gone for up to an hour."

"It could have been. I don't have a watch."

"You said you were angry for him leaving you."

"Too right. You don't go leaving a lass in the middle of nowhere when there's a war on," Kara was now animated as she spoke. "I was going to give him a piece of my mind."

"But you didn't?"

"No, he kissed me when we got back in the car." She paused, hesitating.

"Go on," said the Major as Kara stole a glance at her mother.

"He is a really good kisser and by the time we finished all my anger had gone." She glanced across embarrassedly at her mother who was sat staring in disbelief at the tale that was unfolding.

"Did you come back the same way as you went?" asked the Major.

"I think so. All I know is that we came back up the Respryn road into Bodmin."

"Did you not see any roadblocks or soldiers patrolling?"

"Not one."

"There's a weakness in your defence of the town, I suggest," said the Major turning to the Captain.

"I was led to believe the Local Defence Volunteers were guarding Respryn Bridge and the nearby railway tunnel," replied the Captain. "But if this was a couple of weeks ago there may not have been anyone. I doubt they would get through now."

"Let's hope so," said the Major who then turned his attention back to Kara. "So how long were you out altogether?"

"I suppose about half an hour getting the petrol, maybe an hour's drive, half an hour there and up to an hour back again. What's that? About three hours I guess. I wouldn't know exactly because I don't have a watch."

"And you have no idea where you went?"

"No."

"This is serious. You realise I could have you arrested if you are withholding information."

"Arrest me then," said Kara defiantly.

"Kara!" Her mother gasped.

"You realise the man we are looking for is a murderer. One of those murders committed in this very house. If you are obstructing the investigation you could land yourself before a judge who could sentence you to jail." It was the Major's turn to sound impatient.

"Sounds like you've been judge and jury before the man is in court. Johann was very kind and pleasant to me." Kara's voice rose as she defended the young lodger.

"If you are in league with this man it could turn out very badly for you, young lady." The Captain had joined in now.

"He's only been here a few weeks so how could I be in league with him? How dare you suggest that I have any part to play in the murder you accuse him of?" Kara was riled now.

"Murders, plural."

"I won't stay here and listen to your accusations, mister. Johann is not a murderer!" Kara stood, swished her gown around her, bade the startled officers "Good night" and headed for the door, breaking into sobs as she reached for the door handle.

"Miss Johns," called the Captain as she slammed the door behind her.

"I'm sorry," said Mrs Johns. "I really don't know what to say."

"May I go and have a word with her?" It was Elizabeth. She took the two officers by surprise. She stood up as Mrs Johns nodded. She looked to the Major.

"It can't hurt," he said and, as she made for the door, took the armchair she had vacated. "Call us if you need us."

"Right to the very top of the stairs and on the right," said Mrs Johns. Elizabeth disappeared out of the room leaving an awkward atmosphere behind her.

Elizabeth tapped on the door. "May I come in?" she said opening the door so as not to allow any opportunity for a refusal. The room was bathed with moonlight. The black-out curtains had been drawn back. It was a small square room with the roof sloping in both sides with a small narrow alcove for the window which jutted out of the roof at the front. There was a wardrobe, a dressing table with a chair, and there sat on the bed with her head in her hands was a sobbing Kara. She stole a quick glance to see who it was who had let themselves into her room but made no comment or attempt to rebut the intrusion.

Elizabeth knelt in front of her and put a comforting hand on Kara's bare knee, the front of the dressing gown had parted as she sat and sobbed. Kara looked at her and when she saw no sign of judgement or condemnation took Elizabeth's hand in her own and sobbed again. They just stayed there not speaking for a minute or two.

"Do you love him?" Elizabeth asked gently. Again Kara looked up. This time she met Elizabeth's gaze and nodded. "Tell me about him," Elizabeth said.

"He wasn't like the others," Kara said hesitantly. "I mean, I have walked out with a few soldiers, you know, cheered them up away from home, give them someone to go to the dance or the pub with." Her voice grew more confident as she spoke woman to woman. "Most just like the company, although you get a few who try it on. You know, put their hands where they shouldn't. Not that I always objected if they were handsome. But Johann, he was cheeky when he spoke. A bit more direct and forward than the Tommies, I guess that was because he was foreign and they don't have the British shyness, do they?"

Elizabeth made no comment. She just listened as Kara continued, "But he was always the real gentleman. 'May I have the pleasure of this kiss?' he asked before we kissed for the first time. Then later he would ask in a silly voice like Mrs Mopp on the wireless 'Can I do you now, sir?' and we would kiss. He would make me feel so special."

"Do you know where he is now?" Elizabeth asked. Kara shook her head.

"When did you last see him?"

"I haven't seen him since Monday," said Kara taking a deep intake of breath as she tried hard not to sob again.

"What happened on Monday?"

"He came back to the house and collected some of his things. When I asked him what he was doing, he said he had to go away for a while, but he promised to come back and see me. He seemed in a hurry. I tried to kiss him, you know, long and passionate like, but he only gave me a quick peck, and said he had to go. He went down and out of the back door when one of the soldiers started shouting at him from an upstairs window. And Johann, I can't believe I saw this, Johann took out a gun and shot him. Then Johann ran and that's the last I saw of him. What's he done to make him do something like that? Why did the soldiers make him do something like that? They said afterwards he got away by train, so I don't know where he is now."

Elizabeth looked at the young girl. Her face was tear-stained, her hair was a mess, yet something didn't quite add up.

"Do you know where he came from?" Elizabeth asked changing tack slightly.

"He was from the Netherlands. He was a refugee."

"Are you sure?"

"Why yes! That's what he said when he first arrived."

"How could you tell he was telling the truth?" Elizabeth persisted.

"He had an accent. He said he came across to Falmouth. There have been loads of refugees arriving there. French, Poles, Breton fishermen, Dutch."

"What if he was German?" Elizabeth asked looking intently at Kara for a reaction. Her eyes shot wide for a second, and then she looked down. Elizabeth continued, "He will still have an accent. He may be a spy or something. That would explain why he would shoot the soldier, and why he would shoot the Major who chased him when he tried to stop him escaping on the train."

"No," said Kara, "I don't believe that's true." Her voice nearly cracked with the emotion. She knew she was lying, but who to trust? Could she trust this pretty young woman who'd arrived with the Major.

"The night you went for a drive with him. You know, the night the Major was asking you about downstairs. You know where you went, don't you?"

"No," said Kara shaking her head. She withdrew her hand from Elizabeth's. So this show of friendship was just a ruse to get her to talk. This woman was as bad as the officers down in the front room.

"You went with him when he got there, didn't you? You know exactly what he did." Elizabeth's voice was soft but carried a conviction about it that obviously was troubling Kara.

"Oh why does love have to be such a complicated thing?" Kara thought. She remembered the time she had first met the blonde young man as he waited for her to come down the stairs. She liked his smile and his adoring gaze and so had prolonged her descent accentuating each step to show off her legs to best effect. He had complimented her and she had flirted with him. There was a magnetic attraction to this young man. She was used to soldiers staying at her parent's house and would often accompany them to the dance or to the pictures if they had no one else to take along, but she was drawn to Johann.

She had laughed so much the evening he had joined her mother and her at the tea table. He was great company, polite, pleasant but with an air of confidence around women that she hadn't seen in the usual British Tommy who lodged in the house. She remembered the night she had gone to tease him clothed only in her dressing gown but as she had parted the gown to give him a quick glimpse of her birthday suit she had heard the kitchen door close and her mother's footsteps on the stairs and so had fled back up to her attic room. It was the day after that Johann had asked her to accompany him on some of his journeys. When her shifts allowed she had travelled to Fowey, to Perranporth, to Falmouth and even down to Penzance. He had bought her tickets. She could never have afforded such regular excursions on her wage from the hotel. But it was those journeys that had sown the seeds of doubt in her mind. He only seemed interested in her when there were men in uniform around. She enjoyed being kissed but soon realised while she shut her eyes lost in the moment, he never did. He was always alert, scanning the view or the people behind her. She had tried to change position so he was facing the other way but he always manoeuvred her so he had the view he wanted. Then he always seemed to be scribbling in a little notebook. There was the occasion when they were waiting for a connection at Chacewater station when she had tried to take it from his pocket and he had become angry with her.

However, that was nothing to his anger and discomfort on the train to Padstow last week. She had asked him about his job, about his travels, about his little book. Mr Carlyle, who was also lodging in her parent's house, was in the compartment as well. Johann squirmed and stuttered. He tried changing the topic of conversation but she kept bringing it back making him squirm even more. He kept looking at Mr Carlyle who pretended to be looking at the scenery of the Camel estuary but was obviously taking in every word. Once they had alighted from the train onto the platform, Johann had taken her firmly by the elbow and guided her out of earshot and told her she was a stupid girl and he could take her no further. She would have to catch the next train back to Bodmin and woe betides her if she tried to follow him. She knew she had overstepped the mark, but she had spent the solitary journey back along the Camel valley trying to decide whether the man she had fallen for was up to no good. Was he just a criminal, maybe a spif, or was he seeking out military information that would be of use to the enemy? The more she thought about the places they had visited, the walks they had shared, the photographs he had taken, there was little room for doubt.

Then there was the drive. He had gone through all the back lanes to avoid the checkpoints on the main roads. They had ended up on the south coast. He had parked the car in a gateway, taken a large battery lamp out of the boot and walked across the fields to the little cove. There he had been sending some kind of signal, a message with the flashlight of this giant torch. To her amazement, from the dark horizon someone out at sea had signalled back. She was now certain the young man whom she was smitten with was in league with the enemy. But who to tell? Wouldn't she get into trouble as well? They hung traitors, didn't they? There was one just a couple of weeks ago, the neighbour had said, hung at the Tower of London for spying for the enemy.

Kara had never felt such a tug of emotions. She had fallen for the young blonde man who had arrived with all his charms, but she knew the country where she lived was at war and facing an imminent invasion, and it was clear that Johann was not on the side of those who would be defending Britain. Should she be loyal to the one she loved, or to the land of her birth?

Like all daughters, she had sounded out her mother. Asking cagily what her mother thought of Johann, she received an overwhelming endorsement of his virtues based on the meal they had enjoyed together. When she pressed her about Johann's job, she was told not to ask him too many questions because a lot of people can't say much about what they do especially if it's connected to the war effort. When Kara asked whether she should do something grand to help the war effort, her mother's expression had changed and she had told her that her job at the hotel was doing enough. "Think of all the officers and men you are serving," she had told her. "You know how your father likes hearing all the latest gossip of who's been in and which regiments are in town!" But the biggest surprise had come when Kara had commented that she wanted to help the land of her birth in its hour of need. "England is not the land of your birth," her mother had told her. "We moved here when you were just a small nipper so your father could continue his flying. That infernal Treaty wouldn't let our homeland keep its air force." When Kara had sought to probe this revelation further her mother had closed up saying she had said more than her father would have wanted her to know and Kara should just keep on doing a good job at the hotel. Kara felt truly confused.

Elizabeth's voice penetrated her ruminations. "You do know where you went and what you did, don't you Kara?"

"No, I told the Major I didn't know."

"No, you told the Major that he kissed you when 'we got back in the car'. That means you had got out of the car too, doesn't it Kara?" Elizabeth reached out and lifted Kara's chin so she had to look at her. Her eyes showed a fear that wasn't there a minute ago.

"You know where you went because you went together. You know what he did." Elizabeth was gentle but firm.

Kara knew she had been rumbled. "I can't say. I promised him I would never tell," she muttered between the sobs.

"You know he's German. You know he's a spy. You could hang for that, Kara." Kara dissolved into tears, her whole body shaking.

"You've got to tell us, Kara. Where did you go?" Kara just shook her head, her broken heart aching from the split loyalties. Elizabeth struggled with what to say that would finally prise the truth out of the sobbing girl. She sensed her heart would be telling her one thing, her head another. Reasoning wouldn't work. Appealing to patriotism as the Major had tried to do didn't work. Scaring her with punishment would simply drive her into herself. She had to reach her heart.

"Do you still love him?" she asked. Kara nodded in between the sobs. Elizabeth continued, "Then you've got to help him?"

"How?" said Kara looking up. "What can I do now?"

"There is half the British army looking for him. Tonight he tried to crash through a roadblock. They opened fire on his car."

Kara looked alarmed at this news. She allowed Elizabeth to clasp her hands as they hung limply on her lap. She took several deep breaths. Her hands felt cold and clammy against the soft velvet of Elizabeth's skin.

"He got away, but I saw the car. It had several bullet holes in it. If the army get to him first they will kill him." Elizabeth paused to let her words sink in. "If you truly love him, you will tell the Major, tell me, where he's headed so we can get to him first. That way we can take him alive. He will live. But if you don't say the net will close in on him and they will shoot him like a hunted animal."

There were more sobs and gasps for air.

"You've got to help him. You are the only one that can, Kara." Elizabeth felt emotionally exhausted. 'Goodness knows what this young woman is feeling' she thought. Part of her felt sorry for the lass, but part of her wanted to beat the information out of her. They were talking about the man who had shot her new love, fortunately only a flesh wound, but the intent had been to kill. She knew the Major would only rest when the threat from this enemy was eliminated. Elizabeth didn't know what else to say. There was a long pause.

"We went to Lantic Bay. He signalled to a submarine to come back and pick him up on the high tide one hour before dawn on the 12th." The truth just gushed forth when it finally came. Elizabeth heaved a sigh of relief but was keen to verify as much as she could.

"Signalled? How?"

"He had a flashlight. It was like a huge torch in a box. I had never seen anything like it before, but that's what he had in the boot of the car."

"The 12th, that's today." The realisation suddenly hit Elizabeth. She let go of Kara's hands and stood.

"Where you going?" asked Kara who looked deadly white and pale.

"To help the Major get Johann. Hopefully alive."

"Then I'm coming with you," said Kara.

"Not dressed like that," replied Elizabeth.

"Give me a second," responded Kara standing up and letting the silk dressing gown slide off revealing her kami knickers. They were black, made of silk, with white lace trimmings. They showed off her figure to a tee. Elizabeth raised an eyebrow. 'Perhaps that's how this Nazi spy had spun the head of this young woman,' she thought.

"True French. A soldier brought them back from France for me at Christmas," Kara said seeing Elizabeth's interest.

"Very nice," Elizabeth offered deciding that asking would only be a distraction from the urgent mission in hand. Kara pulled on a pair of slacks and a jumper and picked up a pair of lace up shoes from in front of the wardrobe and said, "I'll put these on downstairs." The two women descended the narrow stairway to the first floor. Kara put an arm on Elizabeth's shoulder.

"Will you tell the Major what I've said? Please, I don't think I could stand him shouting at me," she said her eyes imploring a positive response.

"Yes, I can do that. But there may be more questions he needs to ask that I can't answer. Come on, we've not got a moment to lose."

Elizabeth could hear subdued conversation as she put her hand on the door handle of the front room, twisted it and opened the door. She stepped just inside and Kara knelt slightly behind putting on her shoes. All eyes turned to them as the conversation ceased.

"Lantic Bay for a submarine," Elizabeth said. The Major smiled, while a look of incredulous adulation came over the Captain's face. Mrs Johns went white.

"When they went for a drive, he signalled it to pick him up on the high tide before dawn on the 12th," said Elizabeth, proud that a woman's approach had succeeded in getting the vital information where the two officers had failed. She looked radiant and beamed at the two officers.

"That's today," spluttered the Captain.

"Now we know why he took the train to Fowey," said the Major getting up. "Thank you Mrs Johns, we'll see you again."

"Kara and I will come with you. We may be of some help in finding the place," said Elizabeth her tone suggesting this was not a matter up for negotiation. The Major glanced around the little group as if he was making up his mind and then pronounced, "Okay, let's go."

Kara kissed her totally bemused mother goodbye on the cheek and followed the others out to the Major's car. The Major said to Elizabeth, "You drive; we'll drop the Captain off at the Depot to bring some reinforcements."

"Where is this Atlantic Bay? Somewhere like Newquay I suppose?" asked the Captain.

"Lantic, just an 'l'," replied the Major. "It's on the south coast about a mile east of Polruan. You need to go to Lostwithiel and down the east side of the river. And while you are rounding up some men a phone call to Admiralty at Fowey might be a good move, especially if we are dealing with a submarine." He turned to Kara, "You get in the front with Elizabeth. You might be able to help show the spot when we get there." The Major clambered in the back with the Captain. It was the Captain who spoke.

"Don't take any chances, sir. We will be as quick as we can."

"Don't worry. I shall not be jumping on any trains."

Chapter 19

The moonlight was beginning to fade as Elizabeth drove the Major's car down the lane past Lanteglos Parish Church towards the coast road. Their movement in the early hours had raised an eyebrow or two at the checkpoints when both the soldiers at Lostwithiel and the LDV at Lerryn saw a Major in uniform being driven by two beautiful young women in civilian dress at such an unearthly hour. Only the Major's papers and his accept no nonsense approach had got them through speedily. Elizabeth slowed to a crawl as the lane bent right and uphill. The dimmed headlamps had provided little light to be able to discern the twists and turns of the Cornish lanes. The Major, while anxious to press on, also knew that their speed meant they would not have to wait too long for the Captain's reinforcements.

Elizabeth approached the T junction at the top of the lane. Kara pointed to the right. Elizabeth gently eased the car forward. She didn't want to make too much noise to alert Johann, if he were in this remote place, to their arrival. No one spoke as they drove westwards along the coast road. ·

They had only gone a matter of yards when Kara broke the silence.

"Here," she said, pointing to a gateway. Elizabeth pulled the car off the lane and parked by the gate. The Major frowned. Kara certainly seemed to know where she was for someone who had claimed she did not have a clue where she was on her late night drive with Johann. He wondered just how many times she had been here before. He decided this was not the moment to ask as he could not risk losing her co-operation at this juncture.

"The beach is one field over," Kara said. "There is a little path down to it." The Major peered into the darkness but couldn't make out anything more than the gate. He told Elizabeth to cut the engine and turn off the lights.

"What are you going to do?" Kara asked. The Major wondered the wisdom of revealing his intentions, but replied,

"I'm going to have a look to see if there is any sign of Johann or this submarine or whether you have led us here on a wild goose chase. For your sake, I hope you haven't."

"We'll come with you," said Elizabeth. "Kara can show us just where this path is."

The Major hesitated for a moment, but realised the advantage of having Kara close by. "Fine, but you had better immobilise the car. We don't want him driving off with it and leaving us stranded."

In a flash Elizabeth was under the bonnet and removed the rotor arm.

"How do you know how to do that?" asked Kara who was visibly impressed.

"I've spent too much time on my father's tractor on the farm," smiled Elizabeth thinking what her father might say if he could see her now. She had been his pride and joy. She thought of days on the farm traipsing the fields beside him caring for the animals. She thought of seeing a cow calf for the first time. She recalled being carried on her father's shoulders as they rounded up the sheep. She sensed again the excitement when her father had bought a tractor and her delight at being allowed to drive it as a teenager. She thought of his quiet nodded approval when her young sailor had asked him for her hand in marriage. She recollected his comforting embrace when his parents had called with the news of the loss of their son. She thought of his look of pride when she had arrived home wearing her ATS uniform just one week ago. As for her gallivanting around the Cornish countryside during the night with the Major in pursuit of an enemy agent she could hear his voice saying, "It's highly irregular but that's my girl!"

She gently eased the bonnet back down avoiding any loud or sudden noises.

"All done," she smiled at the Major. He turned and held the gate into the field open for the two women.

"You don't look dressed for the farm," he whispered at Elizabeth as she passed struggling to get her arms in the sleeves of her cardigan.

"I've done far worse," she hissed back at him.

Kara pointed that they should follow the line of the hedge along the side of the field. The sound of the sea as the waves broke on the shore was now clearly audible. The Major drew his revolver, much to Kara's horror, and led the way. Elizabeth indicated Kara should follow and she brought up the rear. She thought it would easier to jump upon Kara if she were to do anything that would endanger the Major should they chance upon their prey.

The field rose slightly before dipping down to where they could make out the line of the bay in front of them. Their eyes were growing accustomed to the darkness and the Major paused to get his bearings. In front of them there was a headland stretching out into the sea. To the right down some steep cliffs was the beach. The cliffs swept round to the right. He knew that the mouth of the river Fowey couldn't be more than a mile or two in that direction but it was not possible to see it from this vantage point. That would most certainly be the direction their quarry was coming from having caught the train to Fowey. The Major assumed he would cross the river. He was unsure what time the last passenger ferry was from Fowey across to Polruan, but he knew their prey would not be averse to stealing a boat to get across if he had missed it. However, he would have had several hours to get himself into the prime position for the pickup. The Major glanced at his watch. He could just make out that it was now a little after three o'clock. The sky would begin to lighten within the hour as the dawn broke across the eastern sky. He knew it was now or never if there was to be a rendezvous. He scanned the sea, looking back and forth from the beach to the horizon and back again several times but there was no sign of a submarine.

'Mind you,' he said to himself, 'it would stay beneath the waves until the very last minute. The chances of picking out a periscope in this light would be extremely limited.'

"Where's the path down to the beach?" he whispered to Kara.

"We have to go over a style in the corner of the field before you come to it," she whispered in reply.

'At least she is still co-operating and has done nothing so far to announce their presence' the Major thought. He waved with his hand indicating they should go on. He led the way following the line of the hedge down to the corner of the field. It had recently been ploughed and the earth was soft beneath their feet on the few occasions he had to step from the hardened path off onto the soil to avoid a bramble protruding from the hedge. The style was made of slate slabs built into the hedge as steps with an upright one on the top to step over. From the top he glimpsed down at the beach but there was no sign of life. He didn't linger too long as he didn't want his profile to be silhouetted against the sky for anyone down on the beach. He turned and held out a hand to help Kara down. She declined keeping her eyes fixed on the revolver in the Major's other hand. He extended the assistance to Elizabeth who took it.

"Just so you don't slip," he whispered. "I know what you are like with styles!" Elizabeth responded by rudely poking out her tongue at him.

They were now stood on the coast path. It had been worn in centuries past by the coastguard patrolling the cliffs to try and prevent smugglers bringing their loot ashore. Lantic Bay, along with many of the small sheltered bays of this stretch of the south Cornish coast, had been ideal for landing cargo that had not paid or would not pay the duty. It would be easy to get it to safe storage before daylight. It was rumoured even the church at Lanteglos had been used before the loot was then given false markings and taken to Polruan and Fowey where it would be easy to sell it right under the noses of the Customs men. Some of the customers were renowned landowners in these parts who didn't ask too many questions as long as they were supplied with the superior quality of French or Spanish liquor. In fact on Pencarrow Head there was the ruin of a hut the coast guard had built for their men knowing that this was such a hotspot.

Once again in time of war and under threat of invasion these paths would be patrolled again, but there was no sign of soldier or Local Defence Volunteer in this remote spot at this hour of the morning. The Major soon spotted the path leading off through the ferns down towards the beach. The three of them silently made their way forward, the sound of the waves breaking on the beach below them seeming extra loud in this tense moment.

"Aargh!" Kara muttered as she pitched into the bracken. The Major spun round in an instant revolver at the ready. He had already determined he might have to use it on Kara if she proved to be in league with the enemy. He was greeted with the sight of her sprawled face down in the ferns with arms outstretched. She gingerly clambered to her feet and brushed herself down.

"Sorry," she whispered. "I tripped." The Major looked around and scanned the beach for any sign of a response. He was not certain that this wasn't some attempt to attract attention. He couldn't see or hear anything other than the waves on the beach. He looked back at Elizabeth. She was eating her fist desperate not to burst into a fit of giggles. She had seen the whole thing and was amused at the Major's reaction to Kara going base over apex on the root of a bush that stuck up as the earth around it had been worn away over time.

The Major frowned. Elizabeth composed herself, took her hand out of her mouth and whispered "Sorry." The Major turned and, after another look down at the beach to check for any sign of movement, began to move forward once more.

Their path bent slightly to the right and then there was a path off to the right. The Major stopped and looked at Kara for confirmation that this was the way down to the beach. She pointed and nodded. They continued down this route which seemed to make its way on to a small headland that divided the beach into two. They were descending quite rapidly now. Just as the path bent round to double back the Major stopped with a start. Kara and Elizabeth stopped, both wondering what he had seen or heard. They looked at him but his gaze was fixed out towards Pencarrow Head where emerging past the headland and coming into the bay was the silhouette against the horizon of a submarine. The women gasped. The Major's mind flashed back to the last time he had seen a German submarine. He was a small boy and had been taken by his parents for a walk along the sea front by the large white Falmouth Hotel. There nestling on Castle Beach were six German submarines. They had surrendered to the Royal Navy at the end of the Great War and had been brought to Falmouth for gunnery practice. Six of them in a gale had been washed against the rocks of Castle Beach below Pendennis Castle. He had marvelled as a boy at the weird and wonderful angles at which they lay as they were left for the sea to take its toll of them.

But this sleek machine was gently manoeuvring into the bay. Its black silhouette stood out from the darkness of the cliffs to the left and the grey of the horizon. She must have been half a mile out from the point, away from the treacherous rocks of the headland that had wrecked many a vessel on this stretch of Cornish coast in days gone by. The Major could feel his heart beating. He turned and looked back at the hill behind them. There was no sign of the Captain or the reinforcements he would be bringing. He looked across the bay to Blackbottle Rock but there was no sign of any boat emerging from Fowey to come to their assistance.

The Major was not an expert on submarines, but he was relieved to see there was no sign of a deck gun on this one. He estimated it must be about 40 yards long. It was in fact a Type IIC. It appeared to be turning, and every now and again above the noise of the surf the Major could catch the sound of a purring 700hp engine. He peered down towards the beach. There was no sight or sound of any movement there. Perhaps they were too late? Maybe the submarine had already made the pick up? But why tarry in this exposed situation?

Suddenly Elizabeth grabbed his arm and pointed back at the submarine. It had stopped moving, its nose pointing into towards the far end of the beach. There was now a flurry of activity on the deck. Several men had emerged from the tower and were manhandling an inflatable dinghy into the water in the lee of its hulk.

Sensing there was not a moment to lose the Major said, "Come on. Let's get down on the beach." He turned and continued on the steep path. In places steps had been cut into the slate rock. The path twisted and turned. At one steep section the Major looked back but the women were carefully picking their way down, so the Major decided to leave them to descend at their own speed. He pressed on until with a final turn he took the last few steps down onto the shingle. The stones crunched beneath his feet in what seemed to him to be a deafening announcement of his arrival on the beach. But the roar of the foot high surf breaking on the sand further down would mean no one more than a dozen yards from the Major would have heard. However, he stood still surveying the scene. There was no one on the beach. He looked along the foot of the cliffs to see if he could make out any shape or form but there were sections which were in complete darkness so he could not be certain who or what was lurking in the shadows.

The Major stepped to the right. He thought he'd stay at the back of the beach hoping that would make his form more difficult to see from the submarine. He looked up but all he could see was the vegetation that covered the steep slope disappearing into blackness until the top of the cliff stood in contrast to the lighter sky. He had gone about ten yards when there was a crunch on the stone behind him. He swung round, revolver in hand, but it was the women who had now arrived at the foot of the path. He waved to them to follow his route and they slowly made their way towards him.

All of a sudden there was a beam of light. It flashed several times, its beam pointing out towards the submarine. It was coming from a rock shelf on the far side of the beach. There was their man signalling to the sub.

The Major waited for the women to catch him up. He now felt very exposed. Perhaps he had been foolhardy and headstrong in rushing down to the beach, especially with two unarmed women. Their quarry would definitely be armed. He had revealed that on several occasions, even using his weapon to fire at unarmed civilians on the railway station, as well as wounding one of the Captain's men back in Bodmin. The men on the submarine would definitely be armed. It would only need one of them to spray the beach with a machine gun and the consequences could be devastating. Perhaps he should have waited while the Captain collected reinforcements? At the very least he could have stayed on the cliff top where the ferns and furze would have provided some cover. He knelt down on one knee, and as the women came to him, they ducked down as well. At least, so far, they had not been noticed. Surprise may be the only thing they had going for them at the moment. Now he knew where his enemy was, the Major pondered his next action. He knew if he were to take a shot he needed to be closer. The effective range on his revolver was limited. But he also wanted the submarine to fully reveal its hand. How many men were going to be coming in the dinghy? He couldn't make it out. He could still see a small cluster of men silhouetted on the deck of the submarine. And if the shooting started, where could he find some cover for the women? Johann was perched on the rock shelf at the far side of the beach. It had provided an elevated platform for him to be able to signal out to the submarine. Between the pursuers and the hunted was an outcrop of rock where the cliff looked like a giant finger pointing down into the sand about to flick this ragged stone marble. It was merely a quirk of the geology which in this section of coast had taken the layers of rock and bent them so they dived into the sand at all sorts of peculiar angles. But it would need daylight for the Major to interpret all the delights of dip and strike at this location. For now, it was one of the areas of darkness where he knew it would be hard for anyone to see shape and form. He motioned to the women to follow him and slowly the three of them scurried, almost bent double, across the tufts of beach grass at the rear of the white sand. They arrived without incident and crouched down again.

"What are you going to do?" panted Kara. It was her question of the hour.

"Watch and pray that the Captain soon arrives," whispered the Major. He didn't add that he was also praying that Kara would not compromise their position in any way. He sensed he could rely on Elizabeth to help out if she did try something, but it would only take a shout or a break from cover for them to lose their element of surprise. Neither did he reveal that as soon as it appeared their man might actually be getting away he would open fire. He thought knowing that would only make Kara more likely to do something reckless for the young man she had obviously fallen for.

The Major peered out to sea. The submarine's deck was washed every now and again with the rise and fall of the swell. There were still several men grouped round the conning tower. The sub must be about 800 yards from where they were. Mid distance he could now make out the dinghy. It had one sailor in it rowing with strong deliberate strokes towards the beach. As the waves rose to break on the beach he was lost from sight for a moment and then appeared again as he crested the next swell.

The Major whispered that the women should wait where they were. He was going to move to the outcrop of rock to get a closer view. Elizabeth nodded. Kara said nothing. Her head was a whirl of conflicting thoughts and emotions. Had she betrayed the one she loved? Had she done the right thing for England? Would their friendship survive the night? Would Johann survive the night? Should she yell and warn him of their presence or would the Major do as Elizabeth had suggested and seek to take him alive? What would happen to him then? She had read in the paper that a German agent had been hanged at the Tower of London. She could not bear the thought of that happening to Johann. Why did the path of true love never run smooth? She shivered as she watched the Major stealthily make his way forward. Elizabeth placed a hand upon her shoulder and smiled. She smiled back not sure whether it was a touch of reassurance or of restraint.

Elizabeth reckoned her companion looked very pale in the dim light. Kara had been very brave leading them to the beach, she thought. But now she was not going to tolerate any move that would cause her beloved Major to be shot again. He had been fortunate on the train in receiving only a flesh wound on the arm. He may not be so fortunate again. She prayed God would look after him, and looked back up at the top of the cliff in the vain hope of seeing the Captain and his men.

The Major was remarkably light-footed for such a tall man as he took small steps deliberately placing one foot in front of the other as he edged towards the rock. When he reached it he turned back flat against it and gave a thumbs-up sign. Elizabeth wasn't quite sure whether he was reassuring them or himself. She watched as the Major turned back, moved to the side and peered over the rock towards Johann.

Suddenly there was a loud crunch on the stones. Elizabeth and Kara jumped. The Major ducked. Johann had come to the edge of the rock shelf and jumped down onto the beach. Elizabeth let out her breath slowly. She glanced at her companion. She was wide-eyed watching Johann but said nothing and made no movement.

The submariner was paddling the dinghy through the breaking surf and with one wave slightly larger than the others came gliding up onto the sand. He jumped out, turned the boat as Johann made his way forward. There was a greeting but Elizabeth didn't understand German so could only guess at what was being said. Johann turned and looked back at the beach. Was he saying goodbye to Cornwall or did he sense there was someone on the beach? The submariner pushed the boat back into the surf and jumped in and took up the oars. Johann pushed him out until he was knee deep. He swung a leg up and into the dinghy. He had one foot in the dinghy and the other in the water when a shot rang out.

The Major had fired. He was leaning round the rock, revolver in hand. He had missed, but the sound of the bullet whizzing past him into the breakers made Johann yell as he heaved himself up and into the dinghy. The submariner strained on the oars. The Major fired again. This time Johann returned his fire sending the Major dodging back behind the rock.

"Johann," screamed Kara as she started to run down the beach towards the departing dinghy. Elizabeth stretched out to seize her but she was gone before her hand could grab her. At least Kara hadn't given them away before the Major had fired. But what was she thinking?

"Johann! Take me with you!" Kara cried. Elizabeth's jaw dropped open. She wanted to yell at Kara but no sound would come out of her mouth. Kara was running for all she was worth. She was past the Major's rock and just a few yards from the water's edge when more shots rang out. Elizabeth could see the Major had again taken a firing position. Kara yelled, her body twisted, her face frozen in a look of shock and pain, and she fell to the ground. Elizabeth gasped. Her mouth went dry. She stared in disbelief. She stood up to move forward towards the stricken girl when a volley of shots rang out from the cliff top. She turned and could simply see a line of muzzle flashes as they fired again. As she heard the rapid purr of a burst from a Bren gun, the Major ran towards her yelling "Get down!" He rugby tackled her to the ground as she heard the whizz of bullets pinging off the pebbles on the beach. The noise was now deafening as it echoed round the cliffs of the bay.

"Sorry," said the Major as they sprawled flat on the beach grass. "The Captain's arrived."

There were pistol shots being fired from the dinghy which was now over the breaking waves and in the swell. The submariner was straining on the oars. The boat suddenly turned sideways for a few yards. Johann continued to fire in the midst of a shower of bullets fizzing into the water around him.

"They've got him!" Elizabeth exclaimed as she saw the boat turn. But as she watched the sailor kept on rowing and then turned the dinghy back in the direction of the submarine.

"What's he doing?" she asked.

"Using the rip current," the Major said as the submariner's strokes now seemed to be taking the dinghy further with each stroke. "The cunning old sea dog," he exclaimed as the realisation dawned upon him their man was going to get away. The firing from the cliff top ceased. None of the bullets had found their target. The dinghy was only visible now and again as it rose on the swell. The men on the submarine were getting ready to receive it. They didn't want to stay around longer than they had to. If the army had been alerted, they knew it would not be too long before the navy would be after them.

The Major stood and ran towards the water's edge letting off the final rounds in his revolver. It was more in anger and frustration than in any hope of hitting the dinghy now.

Elizabeth ran to where Kara's limp body lay on the sand. A bloody stain across her chest, her eyes fixed open in a haunted stare. Life had already flowed from her. Her arms lay where they had flailed, but Elizabeth noticed her right hand was clenched. She gently prised the fingers open to reveal a watch. It had a white face with luminous hands pointing to black numbers. In the middle were the letters K.M. Elizabeth didn't know what they stood for but she guessed this was a present from Johann. She closed the fingers back round it again and laid the hand gently on her chest. The Major turned and came and stood over them.

"You shot her, but not him," said Elizabeth looking up at the officer returning his revolver to its holster. Her statement was more of a question as the anguish on her face revealed. The Major shook his head but said nothing. Elizabeth closed Kara's eyes and just knelt by her in silent prayer. Elizabeth was in shock. She felt angry. She had just witnessed cold blooded murder. An unarmed woman shot in the back by the officer she thought she loved.

She looked up as the sound of boots scrunching on the pebbles approached. It was the Captain and a number of his men.

"Get that Bren to the water's edge and fire on the sub. You may get lucky!" he ordered and several men ran on.

The sound of firing rang round the bay again. Elizabeth put her hands over her ears. It made little difference so all she could do was watch. The dinghy had reached the sub and its occupants were being hauled up on deck. No one returned fire but one by one the figures climbed the tower and disappeared from sight. The 30 round magazine was soon emptied and the men went to reload.

"Cease firing!" bellowed the Captain. "You'll not do any damage at that distance." The submarine's engines could clearly be heard above the noise of the surf. The soldiers stood and watched the black hulk glide away and disappear under the waves. Elizabeth's hands dropped to her side. It was over.

The Captain came and knelt down next to Elizabeth. He looked at Kara and then gently lifted her to look at her back. The old detective mind was at work again. He softly lay her back down on the sand and straightened her arms and legs.

"Shot from the front," he said. "Our man obviously didn't want to take her with him."

"Silence the traitor, more like," replied the Major. "London will be livid he got away. She obviously knew more than she told us. Did you alert the Navy at Fowey?"

"Yes, they were sending out an anti-submarine trawler straight away from Fowey, and were hoping Devonport could send out a couple of Destroyers. He may not get away yet."

"Let's hope so."

Elizabeth stood and steadied herself on the Major's arm. She looked at him and said, "So you didn't shoot her?" The Major shook his head in reply.

"I'm sorry. I thought…" and Elizabeth's voice trailed away.

"Come on," he said gently. "You've seen enough for one night. Let's get you back."

"What about Kara?" asked Elizabeth glancing down at the lifeless form of the young woman.

"My men will sort her out, miss," said the Captain.

"But her parents? Who's going to tell her poor mother? And what will you tell her?" The questions were flooding into Elizabeth's mind.

"We'll take care of business," said the Captain.

The Major put his arm around Elizabeth's shoulders and steered her away. "Come along, we've got quite a climb ahead of us."

Chapter 20

The sunlight warmed the soft slate of the walls of the old parish church. Dawn had seen much of Cornwall shrouded in mist but now by eleven o'clock the sun had broken through. The flagpole on the small tower over the door was empty. At the top of the steps from the Square now painted in a white chessboard pattern to beat the blackout and prevent anyone falling up or down them a few people stood and conversed as they waited for the cortège to arrive.

The Major and the Captain stood talking in hushed tones with Elizabeth looking resplendent in her ATS uniform. She was pleased to have the Major back so soon. He had left on the train on Saturday but returned yesterday for the funeral and to "tidy the whole business up". He had received a frosty reception from Churchill who had been told the news that a German agent had spent a month roaming the Cornish countryside spying on who knows what and then been able to get away from under our very noses. He was astounded that one of the Intelligence Officers overseeing the creation of the Auxiliary Units was among the casualties left in his wake. He had thawed a little when he learned the Major had been wounded in his attempts to apprehend the enemy and was genuinely impressed with the Major's reports on the preparations of Cornwall's defences against the forthcoming invasion. The Prime Minister was a little perplexed that Johann had not used the wireless in any of his communications. It was the eavesdropping on the German signals traffic that had led to a number of agents being successfully captured in other parts of the country, often being met by a reception committee when they landed. This had only made Churchill more certain that Cornwall featured prominently in the German invasion plans. He was happy to send the Major back to Cornwall for a few days to meet the new Intelligence Officer from Plymouth who had made his first visit to the county on Sunday and to see whether Kara's involvement with the German was anything more than a whirlwind romance and to attend the funeral to make sure no untoward rumours would emanate concerning her demise. The Major was delighted that he would see a little more of Elizabeth and hopefully if her duties allowed get to take her out for dinner once more.

The Captain was pleased to receive the Major's news that Churchill had promised his men some new troop carriers to help with their defensive duties on the Bodmin

Stop Line. He had also been instructed to build a small barracks in the woods at Pencarrow for the men to oversee and defend a large emergency arms dump that would supply the troops along the line when the invasion arrived. The government were assured of the co-operation of the landowner. His mansion was already in use as a secret store for sugar supplies for the county of Cornwall. The Captain already had in mind a site for the barracks. He had visited the great house briefly when overseeing the construction of a pillbox at the junction at Mount Charles. To improve the line of fire of the field fortification he wanted to reduce the height of a hedge and as a courtesy had called to inform the landowner of his men's actions. His site for the new barracks was as close to the small hamlet of Washaway as the woods would allow so it would blend in to its surroundings rather than be a new build in the midst of the woodland. The buildings would be at the western end of Rainbow Plantation as close to the school as he could make it. Then German aerial reconnaissance may simply think the building was connected with the school. Obviously he'd store the ammunition at a safer distance into the woods where it would be better camouflaged.

The conversations ceased as the hearse drove across the Square and pulled up at the foot of the steps. A second car pulled up behind it carrying a distraught Mr & Mrs Johns.

"We can't afford that," Mrs Johns had protested when the Captain told her of the arrangements. "We are just simple folk."

"The government will pay for it, Mrs Johns," she had been assured. "As your daughter was killed doing her duty in revealing to the authorities the pick-up point for the submarine, this is one small way we can honour her sacrifice," the Captain had said. He had agreed with the Major to keep their view of Kara's treacherous assistance to the spy from her parents while they watched them and investigated just how loyal this family were to the nation's cause. Only the Commanding Officer at RAF St Eval had been informed so he could keep an eye on aircraft fitter Johns and make sure there was no sabotage on the airfield.

The small procession followed the coffin into the church. It was a grand building, the largest church in the county until the cathedral had been built at Truro sixty years ago. But now the handful of friends and neighbours, a representative from the hotel where Kara worked, and the trio in military uniform looked a pitifully small congregation in such a vast edifice.

The Reverend Young, when all had taken their places, implored God's presence on their gathering and announced the first hymn "The Lord's my Shepherd." From the back of the church the organ burst into life and the congregation sang in doleful voice.

The minister eulogised over the beauty of a vibrant young woman, known to many through her work in one of the town's main hostelries. He condoled the parents on the tragic loss of their only child and made platitudes about us all being God's children. The Major's mind strayed to a land where some of its citizens were certainly not viewed in such a way. Or was it because they were God's children that some people had been singled out?

He reached inside his jacket and took the envelope out of his pocket. He slid the dog-eared photograph out from the letter inside and sat staring at the faces of the family that grinned happily at the camera. It had been taken in more peaceful times. His brother stood behind his seated wife holding their young son on his lap. Where were they now? If only he'd gone straight there? The guilt racked him and he felt his eyes moisten. Would God give him a second chance as Elizabeth had suggested? If only there was word that they were all alright.

"Life was about choices," the vicar's words penetrated the Major's consciousness. "No one knows what choice young Kara was making when she ran towards the one who would end her life so cruelly. No one knows what choice the young man made when he pulled the trigger, but he will have to give an account to Almighty God one day." Perhaps it was the thought of a great reckoning that caused the Major's guilt? Maybe it was the sense of having let down his brother? Or even the haunted feeling he had whenever he closed his eyes and could see the tortured face of his mother when he returned to say he could not find her eldest son and his family?

He felt a hand slip under his arm and hold him. Elizabeth was looking down at the photograph. She said nothing but squeezed his arm. He replaced the photograph and returned the envelope to its place near his heart. Elizabeth smiled gently at him, her eyes full of sympathy.

The congregation suddenly stood, heads bowed. The Major had missed the instruction for them to say the Lord's Prayer. He stood and listened to the words. "Forgive us our trespasses as we forgive those who trespass against us." How can a parent who's lost an only child to the bullet of an enemy spy who had beguiled their daughter into falling for him and then when she was demonstrating her love in the moment of crisis shot her in cold blood utter such words? An eye for an eye and tooth for a tooth was what the Major had learned as a young boy. That made much more sense. That's why he was fighting the enemy. That's why he hated everything they stood for. There was a lot about this faith of Elizabeth's that he just couldn't fathom. Yet there she was in uniform next to him, a kindred spirit in the fight. He respected her but he knew he had a long way to go in ever trying to understand her.

The congregation were singing again. The Major mused over the words in the hymn book.

"Under the shadow of Thy throne, Thy saints have dwelt secure; Sufficient is Thine arm alone, And our defense is sure."

The words turned the Major's thoughts to the mission that had brought him to Cornwall. They were certainly building all manner of fortifications to repel the invader. The Bodmin Stop Line with its combination of natural geography, fortifications and anti-tank islands would certainly do its best. But was the defense sure? Would it be the British faith in God and their sense of fighting a just cause that would see them successfully standing alone against the armies of tyranny and oppression? Would that be enough? What else was there? How do you oppose what is evil except with that which is good? 'You can only stop wrong with right,' he recalled his grandfather saying. Right now, he thought, Britain would take anything that would keep the Nazi hordes the far side of the Channel.

He felt a tug on his sleeve. The service had finished and Elizabeth was making sure he followed her as they processed out behind the mourning parents. He blinked as they stepped out into the bright sunlight. They stood by the old priory pillar as they watched the coffin be carried down the steps to the waiting hearse. The Captain stood by the church door with a couple of soldiers who had arrived from the Depot.

"Are you alright?" asked Elizabeth when she felt no one was nearer enough to overhear. "You were a million miles away in there."

"Let's leave them to their grief. I don't think we'll go to the cemetery," the Major replied. "Let's go and find somewhere for a cup of tea."

"Zac, that sounds like a wonderful idea," said Elizabeth smiling.

"Let's try Lean's Licensed Refreshment House over there on the corner," said the Major. The family run café stood on the corner at the bottom of Turf Street. They waited at the top of the steps as the hearse drove off round the corner, and then descended arm in arm and crossed the Square.

Elizabeth had just stirred the teapot and was pouring out two cups of tea when the Captain came into café.

"I saw you disappear in here. Mind if I join you?" the Captain asked as he pulled out a chair at their table.

The Major called for an extra cup and saucer and Elizabeth poured an extra cup of tea.

"I saw you were talking with two of your men so we thought we'd leave you to it," said the Major when the proprietress had disappeared back into the kitchen.

"You'll be interested in what they had to say. The Depot has just received a report that the LDV found a rubber dinghy this morning washed up at Talland Bay a few miles up the coast from the beach. Three of its inflatable sections were flat due to bullet holes. You were closer to getting him than you thought."

"Yes, that's as maybe, but no word from the navy on that submarine," said the Major sipping his tea.

"The only thing they found in the dinghy was rather strange," said the Captain with an air of mystery.

"Go on," said the Major leaning closer.

"A top hat."

"A top hat," repeated the Major. His face was a mixture of surprise and perplexion.

"Yes, an English gentleman's top hat. Or as the report described it 'A top hat like those Mr Chamberlain was accustomed to wearing.'"

"How bizarre!" exclaimed Elizabeth.

"Is it some kind of calling card? It certainly didn't seem to be Johann's. He had nothing like that with him on the beach. Only the signal lamp." The Major scratched his head.

"Must have come from the submarine then," said the Captain. "Any way it was reported as 'wet and soggy' and is unlikely to be fit for wearing again."

The trio chuckled and swapped funny hat stories as they polished off the pot of tea.

————————

The platform was wet from the morning rain as the passengers hurried to board the 11:38 for Plymouth. A porter was loading parcels from his trolley as quickly as he could but the rain was dripping off the peak of his cap and he stopped to take it off, shake it before replacing it on his head. The Castle-class locomotive "Pendennis Castle" stood gleaming in the rain which had provided her with her first decent clean in weeks. She had been busy pulling troop trains along the Great Western's lines from her home at Oak Common. She was a rare visitor to Bodmin though, but having brought a train down yesterday, she spent the night at St Blazey before being assigned to work her way back up east pulling the local to Millbay in Plymouth, and then an hour later the express to Paddington. The fireman was busy building up the steam and although the first part of the run down to Bodmin Road was all downhill he knew he would need the power to haul the train up through the Glynn valley.

Stood under the station canopy, just outside the waiting room, were a young couple in military uniform. As they embraced few took any notice. It was a scene which had played out on numerous platforms across the country as the nation had gone to war. The couple only had eyes for each other.

"Do come back at the very first opportunity," said Elizabeth.

"Surely the fact that I've had these few days down in Cornwall shows you I won't hesitate to return," replied the Major.

"I know. It's been wonderful. But it goes past so quickly," said Elizabeth pulling him closer and laying her head on his shoulder. He gently kissed her forehead.

"At least dinner last night proved to be a quieter do than the previous occasion we had dined together," mused the Major.

"Oh Zac, it was wonderful," gushed Elizabeth thinking not of the food at the hotel, but the hour they had spent together in the Major's car parked on a patch of grass just off the road to Launceston on a hill on the moor as they watched the sunset over the western skyline. They had not seen another soul, just a few curious sheep who had wandered around the car for a while. For ages they had just sat and held hands and talked and talked. Then the Major had moved closer, leaned across and kissed her, and she had just swooned in his passionate embrace and wished the moment would never end.

"I'll write and I'll send you all my loving every week," the Major said knowing he would miss Elizabeth as desperately as she him, but it wasn't exactly the manly or soldierly thing to admit it.

"Don't you forget," said Elizabeth glancing up at him, her blue eyes smiling.

"You have stolen my heart, my sister, my bride; you have stolen my heart with one glance of your eyes. How delightful is your love," said the Major softly.

"That's beautiful. Is that a poem you wrote?" asked Elizabeth amazed at a new facet of this intriguing man. The Major laughed.

"No, I could never write anything that beautiful. It's the words of Solomon written some two thousand eight hundred years ago. But you smile with your eyes and I have fallen in love with your eyes, with your smile and with every part of you."

Elizabeth lifted her head and kissed the Major on the lips. He embraced her and the kiss became passionate, the joining of two souls.

"Ahem!" The loud cough startled them and they pulled apart suddenly.

"Excuse me sir, miss. The train is about to leave. You need to board now if you're going," said the porter.

"Thank you very much," said the Major who could feel his cheeks flushed red as if he'd been caught like a naughty schoolboy stealing a kiss behind the pavilion on the sport's field.

"I love you," said Elizabeth brushing an imaginary piece of fluff off the Major's lapel. "Do take care."

"Ditto," said the Major. He stepped up into the carriage and shut the door, pulled down the window and leaned out for a final kiss as whistles seem to come from both ends of the platform. The guard, whistle in mouth, stood waving his green flag. The engine driver gave another shrill blast on the engine's whistle and eased off the brake to allow the engine to begin to pull forward. Enveloped by clouds of steam and getting drenched from the steady rain Elizabeth stood waving until the train disappeared from sight under the road bridge at the far end of the station cutting. Already her heart ached with longing for the Major's return. She turned and walked back along the platform to head back to the Depot and whatever duties Sergeant Buscombe would load upon her in return for being allowed this hour off so that the other ATS girls would see that such favours did not come lightly. 'It was a small price to pay,' she thought as she stepped over the torrent of rainwater gushing down the gutter and crossed the road. She saluted at the gate, showed her pass and disappeared into the Keep.

EPILOGUE

The reflection of the forest was shimmering on the surface of the lake as Johann stood at the open cottage window looking out across the Oderteich. The mountains, rising above the tips of the firs, stood majestic and timeless.

How peaceful it all was. So unlike the beach he had escaped from on the Cornish coast. He knew he was lucky to be here as bullets had pierced the dinghy on either side of him but remarkably had not hit either him or the sailor sent to rescue him.

He thought of Kara. How stupid of her to think she could have come with him. She brought her death upon herself he told himself. He could not have let her divulge to the English just where he had been and what he had been doing. After the invasion he would personally see to it that the Major was eliminated. That was how he would avenge the death of the pretty young girl who in helping screen his mission had very nearly caused it to fail. Yes, that's what he would do. He would feel better about it all then.

"Come and sit down, my boy. I have cooked your favourite. You must be hungry after your journey from Berlin." It was Johann's grandmother, delighted to have her favourite grandson to fuss over again.

"Schnitzel!" exclaimed Johann eyeing what was on the plate. He smiled at his grandmother and sat down at the large pine table on the far side of the room.

"There, you get that down you. Then you can tell us all about your visit to the Fuhrer."

"There's not much to tell. I was ushered into this room in the Chancellery. He was sat behind a desk at the far end. He rose and came round the desk, shook my hand. He said he was delighted I had made it back, that I had served the Fatherland well and then pinned the Iron Cross on my chest."

"So brave, my little Johann," said his grandmother patting him on his head as he took another mouthful of the veal.

"Less of the little, please," he smiled as he chewed.

"But brave. Did you get this medal for fighting in France?" she asked. Johann looked around the room before answering.

"England, Oma," he replied. "But you must not tell anyone that. It's top-secret." Then Johann's grandfather spoke up for the first time,

"You don't tell me that little corporal is going to try and invade England now?"

"That's what my mission was about. Collecting intelligence ready for the invasion. I certainly caused no small stir. England's days are numbered."

"Doesn't he realise the Spanish tried and failed, Napoleon tried and failed? I suppose he thinks the German army can walk on water across the Englisch-Kanal."

"It's not good to talk about the Fuhrer in such a way, Opa," warned Johann, concerned he had perhaps told his grandparents a little too much.

Grandfather grunted. "Who's going to hear me out here in the mountains?"

"Will you have to go back?" his grandmother asked her voice full of concern. She had seen too many young men suffering due to war twenty five years ago to want her grandson to number amongst the casualties of this conflict.

"Possibly. I have to report back to Tirpitzufer on Monday once my week's leave is up."

"Well, mein Enkel, you enjoy your Scnitzel while you can. I'll go and put the kettle on for some coffee."

HISTORICAL NOTE

While I have made every attempt to make the background for this story as accurate as possible, any interpretation or representation of historical figures or events, whether national or local, is purely mine based upon the available sources. The main characters and their actions are the creation of my imagination as this is a work of fiction. For example the 8th Worcestershire Battalion did come to Cornwall and built many defences especially around Falmouth. I have them arriving a month earlier than they actually did to give a backstory to Captain Cregoe.

Cornwall did feature in the German invasion plans. It was singled out in Hitler Directive No 16. The Germans were aware of Cornwall's strategic importance both in terms of its geographical location in dominating the Western Approaches and in communications given its cable and wireless links to the rest of the Empire and the United States. The British government took the threat seriously. The War Cabinet Minutes for the Chief of Staff's Committee dated 26th August 1940 show discussion of and response to a report from the Military Attaché in Washington of a German plan to land a force from rubber boats in South West England with the object of cutting off Devon & Cornwall and then advancing up the Severn basin and down the Thames basin, thus cutting off the south of England.

The premise of German agents landing in Cornwall is real. In the early 1990s I spoke with a member of the Home Guard who told me the story of two dead Germans being found on the upper reaches of the River Fal in a rubber dinghy in the summer of 1940. I have simply added a third to create my spy. The notion of German submarines sending people ashore is also based on real accounts from early in the war such as the occasion a German submarine captain anchored off Porth Nanven and sent two crewmen ashore to successfully replenish the vessel's supply of drinking water.

Cornwall was amongst the first places to suffer civilian casualties from enemy air raids even before the recognised start date for the Battle of Britain. The air raid on Falmouth Docks described in the novel occurred on the 10th July 1940 and was the 8th raid the town had suffered. A more detailed historical account can be found on the YouTube channel 'Phil in Cornwall'. Falmouth by the time of its final raid on 30th

May 1944 had sounded the alert 783 times. For comparison, West Ham in the east end of London and at the heart of the Blitz had 1227 alerts during World War Two, and Plymouth, according to figures issued in 1947 by the Town Clerk's Office, had 602 alerts. For several months in 1941 Cornwall was the most bombed county in England. Fortunately it did not suffer the huge loss of life experienced elsewhere, but the impact of a handful of deaths in small rural communities can seem as devastating.

The wartime locations of the Bodmin Stop Line used are real, but of the few that survive, most are on private land and should only be viewed with permission. Few documents survive in the National Archives, and there is little published literature or reference in Museums to the Bodmin Stop Line. To correct this imbalance, compared to its more famous compatriots, was one of the reasons for choosing this location for my novel.

I trust this novel will have provoked you to getting out the map, looking up places and choosing to visit some of the towns and villages mentioned and to researching the reality of the wartime experience in the most westerly tip of the country. Cornwall is enchanting and you will find it so for yourself.

THINGS TO DO

For more on Cornwall in World War Two check out the YouTube channel 'Phil in Cornwall'. Here you will find numerous video-book style presentations of places and events in Cornwall during the war, with some documenting the remains that are still standing today. These videos started as the by-product of the research for this book.

Some places you may like to consider visiting:

The Porthcurno Telegraph Museum with its wartime tunnels;

Pendennis Castle, Falmouth;

Cornwall's Regimental Museum at Bodmin;

The RAF Davidstow Moor Memorial Museum at Davidstow;

The Cornwall at War Museum at Davidstow;

Trebah Gardens with its D-Day Embarkation Hard on the Helford River;

St Eval Parish Church with its memorials to those who flew from RAF St Eval;

The numerous small museums dotted around the county in places like Padstow, Bodmin, Fowey, Wadebridge, Liskeard, Launceston, Helston, Constantine, St Agnes, Liskeard, Lostwithiel, Looe, Mevagissey, Newquay, Perranzubuloe in Perranporth, Redruth, Saltash, Penryn and St Ives as well as the Royal Cornwall Museum in Truro and the Heritage Centres at Grampound, Gerrans, Bude, Callington, and Hayle are all well worth a visit. There is one near you so there's no excuse!

For the rail enthusiast you can still ride on parts of some of the branch lines described in the novel. Visit the Bodmin & Wenford Railway at Bodmin General Station and the Lappa Valley Railway for a narrow gauge ride along part of the Chacewater to Newquay branch line.

And finally while you may still have members of your family who were alive during the war record their memories and tales – you will never regret it. Grasp their stories before it's too late.

COMING SOON

"No Small Stir" is the first book of a trilogy involving Major Trevennel, Elizabeth Treluckey and the German agent Johann.

The next book set a little later in the war will feature the work in Cornwall of the Radio Security Service, sabotage in the dockyard and also the 'last casualty of the Bismarck' attacked in Cornish waters in 1941.

The third will feature the build-up of American forces in the county prior to D-Day in 1944 when racial tensions from the States were played out in a number of Cornish towns.

The trilogy will reveal more of Major Trevennel's inner turmoil over his family as well as tracing the ups and downs of his relationship with Elizabeth.

Keep your eyes and ears peeled for news of their publication dates.

FURTHER COPIES OF THIS BOOK

may be purchased from your local bookshop

or from

nosmallstiruk2017

on Ebay.